JOSEPH O'NEILL was born in Cor[illegible] He is the author of three novels – *Netherland*, which was longlisted for the Man Booker Prize and wo[illegible] PEN/[illegible]ulkner Award for Fiction, *The Breezes*, and *This Is th[illegible]* – and a family history, *Blood-Dark Track*. A barrister in London for many years, he now lives in New York.

From the reviews of *The Breezes*:

'What is the correct response to random tragedy? This dilemma is at the heart of Joseph O'Neill's fine second novel. O'Neill's considerable achievement is to render all these disasters at once deeply affecting and extremely funny. This is a novel about losers forced to become winners, and it works'
Guardian

'A hilarious chronicle of life's crappiness. O'Neill captures our peculiar mannerisms and shifting moods with style and precision, and his depictions of the moments when hilarity drifts into hysteria are always brilliant' *TLS*

By the same author

Netherland
Blood-Dark Track: A Family History
This is the Life

JOSEPH O'NEILL

The Breezes

HARPER PERENNIAL
London, New York, Toronto, Sydney and New Delhi

Harper Perennial
An imprint of HarperCollins*Publishers*
77–85 Fulham Palace Road, Hammersmith, London W6 8JB

www.harperperennial.co.uk
Visit our authors' blog at www.fifthestate.co.uk
Love this book? www.bookarmy.com

This Harper Perennial edition published 2009
1

First published in Great Britain by Faber and Faber Ltd in 1995

A catalogue record for this book is available from the British Library

ISBN 978-0-00-730923-8

Printed and bound in Great Britain by Clays Ltd, St Ives plc

THE BREEZES

1

Fourteen years ago my mother, whose name was Mary Elizabeth Breeze, was killed by lightning, and you may think that my father's quota of misfortune would have been used up once and for all on that violent afternoon. If so you are mistaken, because these last days' events have slapped and hammered and clobbered him around in the way that certain absurd cartoon characters are by their creators. I have particularly in mind the tragedy of the coyote – Wile E. Coyote, he is called – who is doomed perpetually to hunt down a maddening desert bird, a roadrunner, and perpetually to fail in the most painful and disastrous fashion. Every one of Wile E. Coyote's stunts rebounds on him, and every episode sees him reduced from a healthy animal to a steaming pile of charred, exploded fur at the bottom of a cliff. The terrible thing is that there is nothing the coyote can do to avoid this fate; no matter how faultless his stratagems, he will always be undone by a circumstance beyond his control – the animators' desire to inflict upon him the maximum of defeat and humiliation. This is how it has felt these last days: my father's misfortune has been so extreme, so capricious, that he could be the victim of some invisible, all-powerful tormentor. I should say that by *misfortune* I do not just mean setbacks pure and simple, those ordinary hardships that attach to us all as inevitably as shadows. I mean freakish reverses. I mean those blows that are, above all, bad luck – that are, as the dictionary puts it, *evil accidents*.

Take, for example, what happened this morning.

It was raining and I was tramping across the graceless heath that unfolds between the western outskirts of this city – the city of Rockport – and the bare hills that loom over it to the west. Crooked white lines on the heath painted out twenty-two bumpy and undersized football pitches, all of which were overcrowded with the slow throngs of footballers. A gale was blowing in fierce gusts, spraying the downpour over the sportsfields in erratic blasts. Goalkeepers froze in the mouths of the orange-netted goals; strikers lingered numbly around the penalty boxes, unresponsive to the shouts of the onlookers. I walked in the direction of the farthest field of all, the one boundaried by the road into the city, and minutes later, burying my chin in my coat and stamping my feet, I joined the spectators on the touchline – nine people and one dog – and began watching the game.

It was not a great match. Two unskilful teams – one in green, one in blue – were chasing after a white football with little success. The big problem was the wind: every time a pass was struck, a swerving gust would swing its phantom boot and propel the ball out on to the road, bringing the traffic screeching to a standstill and forcing yet another delay in play as a sodden figure slowly went to retrieve it.

Then I noticed something else. In their frustration, the players had started to foul each other, exchanging bodychecks and clattering, metallic late tackles; and as the fouls went unpunished, so the violence escalated: now a defender kneed a jumping attacker in the back, now someone retaliated by shoulder-barging the defender to the ground and now, right before my eyes, someone else threw a punch at the barger. This was mayhem. This game was completely out of control.

'Ref!' the man next to me shouted. 'Ref! Get a grip of it, you blind bastard!'

'Send him off!' a woman screamed. 'For Christ's sake, send him off!'

I looked out for the referee. His face grey with exertion, his tongue a dab of yellow in his open mouth, he was jogging desperately up and down the field, trying to keep up with play – a Sisyphean struggle; each time he caught up with the ball someone would kick it right back to where he had come from.

Just then came a crack and one of the greens was rolling on the turf, hacked down by one of the blues. Puffing thin peeps on his whistle, the referee arrived, panting and struggling for something in his pocket.

'Look here,' the referee said, breathing heavily, 'I – I saw that.' He took another deep breath and pointed into the distance, at a dressing-room of his imagination. 'Do that one more time and . . .'

At that moment the dog ran on to the field. It made straight for the referee and – there is, unfortunately, no more accurate description – began to fuck his left leg. Yes, that is what actually happened: a skinny mongrel sprinted up to the ref, grabbed his thigh tightly between its paws, and started thrusting at his knee with its slippery pink dick out there for all to see. The referee tried to shoo the dog away, but the dog – a terrier of some kind, with tenacity in its pedigree – would not back down. Hopping relentlessly along on its hind legs, it just kept right at it. Trying to shake his leg free, the referee suddenly slipped, landing badly on his behind. Everybody burst out laughing. Spread-eagled in the mud with the dog still writhing on his leg, the derision of the crowd and the players roaring in his ears, anguish and dirt all over his face, the ref blew for time.

That was Pa. The referee was Pa.

I have to say, before I dwell further on this outrage, that there exists a perfectly rational explanation for it. The reason that mutt went for Pa is that he has a dog of his own, a basset hound called Trusty, who is in heat, and clearly some of her love scent had perfumed him. That dog is a minx. After two years of cohabitation, my father is still trying to house-train her. For one thing, she still shits around the home. Although Pa has followed the training manual (*The Wolf in Your Home*) and chastised her while simultaneously pushing her snout into the dung, Trusty has never quite put two and two together and made the connection between the offence and the punishment; or, if she has, she has not let it bother her, a profound canine instinct informing her, correctly, that my father's threats are as insubstantial as the breath that transports them. Either way, he still spends a lot of time on his hands and knees, scraping up. The only effect of his remonstrations, as far as I am able to tell, has been to make Trusty more wily in her choice of location. Whereas in the past she used to squat down on the deep-pile carpet in the living-room, now, like a *grande dame* caught short in the palace of Versailles, she tends to climb up the stairs and do it in rarely visited corners and recesses. If you go round to

Pa's house you have to watch your step. Trusty has toilets everywhere.

But let me return to what happened to Pa at the football. My father's tumble would under normal circumstances have had some slapstick joke value, because, and let me say this at once, I find downfalls as funny as the next man. If some clown vanishes down a manhole or lands face-first in a cream cake, I'll slap my thigh along with everybody else. But for once I am not laughing.

Again, I have to think of Wile E. Coyote – more precisely, of his adventure with the tunnel. The coyote, tired of outlandish artifice, comes up with a scheme which is cunning simplicity itself. Using paint, he depicts a road tunnel on the face of a mountain and then hides behind a boulder, lurking. The plan is obvious: the roadrunner will mistake the fake, super-realistic tunnel for an actual one and will crash into the mountain at great speed. As usual, the plan is about 75 per cent successful. Sure enough, along comes the roadrunner in a fast cloud of dirt and, yes, up it storms, straight towards the picture of the cavern; but then, instead of rebounding off the rock, the roadrunner goes *through* it – through the nonexistent tunnel! For a second or two the prairie wolf gapes at us, crushed and flabbergasted; but then a what-the-hell, ask-questions-later expression animates his crumpled features and, yellow-eyed and ardent, off he races, arms outstretched and hands grabbing, hot on the heels of the bird – and thuds face-first into the mountainside.

It is then, at the moment when he is slumped in a dazed heap at the bottom of the mountain, that the true dismality of his predicament dawns on Wile E. Coyote: that, even where the laws of nature are concerned, there is one rule for him and another for the roadrunner. It is the ultimate unfairness.

I am not suggesting that what is happening to Pa breaks the laws of material physics. But it does break what I always vaguely understood to be another law of nature: the law of averages. I was always under the impression that the law of averages meant this: in the long run, probability will operate so as to effect a roughly equitable distribution of chance – you lose some, but you also win some. But what if you lose some and then, against all the odds, lose some more – and then more still? Where does that leave the law of averages? Where does that leave Pa?

This is what I was puzzling over on the bus here. My head was poised heavily on the rain-steamed window as I sat there, slowly grappling with this enormous problem. And then the penny dropped: there is no such thing as the long run. My father's life is too short to allow probability to take effect.

The vibrations of the bus banged my head against the pane.

Now, I can see a response to this: people make their luck.

To a certain extent, this is right. You make your own bed and you lie in it. But sometimes you are forced to lie in a bed which you did not make at all. No, it is worse than that: sometimes a bed you have never seen before in your life will crash through the ceiling and flatten you before you even know what's hit you. How much of his lot has Pa brought on himself? Merv – did Pa bring Merv on himself?

I received the telephone call at home on Friday morning. Pa asked me how I was and, before I could answer, I heard a swallowing noise – a literal, phonic *gulp*.

I said, 'Pa?'

There was a pause, and then Pa said quickly in a thick voice, 'Listen, son, do you remember Merv, Merv Rasmussen?'

Of course I remembered Merv. He was one of Pa's best friends, his work buddy and tennis partner. I had met Merv plenty of times.

Pa said, 'He was driving along last night, just driving along on his side of the road, minding his own business, when this car just ploughs straight into him. Head-on. Just like that.' Pa took a swallow of wonder. 'This guy just swings across into his lane, then . . .' Here his voice crumpled. I heard it again – *gulp*.

I said, 'Is he going to be all right?'

'I don't know,' Pa said. 'The hospital told me he was critical.'

Critical was the last word I would have associated with Merv. Merv was friendly, tolerant and condoning. As far as I knew, Merv had never passed an adverse judgement on anyone in his life.

Pa said softly, 'Johnny, I want you to do me a favour. I want you to pray for him.' He was serious. 'Just a quick prayer, that's all. I'm telling you, son, right now he needs all the help he can get.'

I did not want to upset my father. I said, 'OK, Pa. I will.'

He took a long and violent drag of air, as though surfacing from a long spell under water. His anxiety made his voice clean and eager. On the telephone, Pa can sound like a young man.

He changed the subject. 'Have you switched the locks yet? Have you spoken to Whelan?'

'Don't worry, Pa,' I said. 'It's under control.'

'I want double locks on that front door,' my father stipulated. 'And tell Whelan to fit one of those big bolts, the ones you can't just kick down.'

'I will, Pa,' I said.

'Ask him about installing an alarm,' Pa said, his sentences beginning to accelerate. 'I want one of those alarm systems that are hooked up to the police station. I want an entry system, too, with a special code, and a spyhole in the door so you'll see who's coming.'

'OK, Pa.'

'I want you and your sister to be safe in that flat,' Pa said. 'And don't worry about the money. I'll take care of that.'

'OK, Pa,' I said – this despite the fact that there is plainly no need for this kind of security at the flat I share with my sister Rosie, which has double-glazed windows which explode when punctured, an impenetrable front door and a film of burglar-proof plastic on every pane of glass. Besides, even if some crook did break in, his pickings would not be rich. Whatever else our flat might be, it is no Aladdin's cave. But I went along with Pa because I had learned that once he is gripped by a sense of imperilment in respect of his family – which is often – he will not be deflected. This is why we Breezes are insured against every imaginable risk. Pa has taken out a comprehensive family protection package that defends the three of us against the consequences of fire, theft, death, sickness and personal injury, of litigation, lock-outs, flooding, explosions, automobile collisions and war, of aviation mishaps, professional negligence, spatial fall-out, forgery, business interruptions and acts of God. You name it, we're indemnified against it.

My father's precautions do not end there. In order to guard against the tax detriments of his own death, he has ploughed as much cash as he can into an accumulation and maintenance fund in his children's names and he has transferred to me, as a nominal gift, the ownership of the flat we live in. 'In case I die within the next seven years,' he said. I told him he was crazy. 'What are you talking about? Seven years? You're never going to die in the next seven years,' I said. I put my hand on the curve of his shoulder, rounded like a rock worn smooth by years of water. 'A fit man like yourself? Why should you?'

'I could go any minute,' he said, clicking his fingers. 'Just like that.' He gave me a look. 'What are you looking so shocked about? That's how it is, son, here today and gone tomorrow, and there's no point in fighting it.'

One reason that Pa so often feels us to be threatened is that he believes that any adversity which befalls someone else is the prognostic of a Breeze adversity. This explained his present concern: having read about an unpleasant burglary in the neighbourhood (a case where the intruders had thrown acid in the face of the elderly woman who opened the door, blinding her), he was determined to take extra measures to ensure our safety.

'Light, Johnny, light!' he exclaimed suddenly. 'Johnny, here's what you do: you get Whelan to install floodlights around the house so that you don't get any shadows out there. You know what they say, a shadow is a burglar's best friend. Yes,' Pa said, 'floodlights. With electronic triggers. My God, when I think of your sister alone at home, and those men lurking about outside her window . . .' He lost his voice.

'Take it easy, Pa,' I said.

Pa resumed, his voice straining, 'Remember, Whelan's the man you want. Ring Whelan. You can count on Whelan.'

'Leave it with me, Pa,' I said. I did not tell him that twice already I had rung Whelan, twice Whelan had promised to come and twice Whelan had let me down. Pa had enough to worry about without worrying about Whelan. Thinking about it, there was not a significant aspect of his life that did not have him on tenterhooks. Everything gave him cause for keen suspense: work, where his job was under review; Rosie and her boyfriend, Steve; Merv Rasmussen; and me. Yes, Pa was losing sleep over me, too, the poor bastard. For three years now I have been one of the reasons why he gets out of bed in the mornings with black rings under his eyes.

Pa's eyes. Among the traits which I am anxious not to inherit from my father, the eyes feature prominently. I roll off the sofa, walk over to the mirror resting on the fireplace and regard myself. What I am looking for is any sign that my eyeballs are losing their alignment. Pa has a wall-eye – a lazy eye. The left eye points in the correct direction but the other eye, the lazy one, looks about a foot to the right. In this respect, Pa has been unlucky. The divergence of his gaze is sufficient to confuse the onlooker, but not quite marked enough to reveal quickly to him which eye is the focused one. To obscure this defect, Pa has taken to wearing tinted glasses, phototonic shades which darken or lighten in accordance with the air's luminousness. The ploy has not come off for him. I am afraid that the main effect of Pa's shades and the just-visible wall-eye beneath them is to give him an insecure, shifty air.

I light a cigarette and for a moment watch myself smoking. Then I look closely at the eyes: still, I am glad to say, perfectly parallel.

However, I have seen photographs of the young Pa. At my age, his eyes were straight as arrows. The famous honeymoon portrait of him and Ma in Donegal shows it clearly: cheek to cheek with his brand-new, bursting, laughing wife, his shirt white and pressed and his tie knotted cleanly, Pa flies the camera a dead-on, bull's-eye of a look, a look that has not the merest trace of a swerve. I know what this means: any day, without warning, some sleeping Breeze gene could wake up and order one of my eyes to make a sideways move.

I turn away from my reflection. There is no point in worrying about it, because there's another paternal characteristic I can do without: the tendency to live in dread. I do not want to end up with a pockmarked, crack-lined face and a head of blitzed white hair. Come to think of it, I do not want to end up like Pa at all. Like father, like son is the last thing I want to hear in connection with me and my father.

2

Angela promised to meet me here, at her flat, at nine o'clock. It is now ten past nine. Ten minutes' delay may not sound like very much, but Angela is as punctual as they come. By her standards, she's late.

I go over to the windows, which stretch extravagantly from the floor to the high ceiling. It's a foul night, the rain violently connecting with the tarmac and spinning like tinsel in the beam of the lampposts. Not to worry. Any minute now I'll hear that struggle with the door, that clatter of things falling to the ground and that dramatic sigh of relief – and then in she'll come, wet and breathless and ready to be held.

I return to lie down on the sofa; and I cannot help but think of Steve, the master of recumbency. Steve lives with me and Rosie in the flat that Pa bought for us. In the days before the flat, Steve and Rosie were sharing cramped rooms at the top of a high tower block and it was generally agreed that, spiritually, financially and geographically, Rosie was going nowhere. Steve was identified as a factor in her malaise and one of the ideas behind buying the new place was that she would be able to come down from that tower block and start afresh.

'You wait and see,' Pa promised. 'It'll be a new leaf for her, just mark my words. There'll be no stopping that girl now,' he said, raising his arm in an upward motion to suggest a rising aeroplane. That was the plan: he would buy the flat and Rosie would leave stranded Steve and all he stood for and remove like a jet into the blue atmosphere.

The change of address almost did the trick. Rosie did get a job – and as an air stewardess, it so happened – but when she and I moved into the new flat, somehow Steve tagged along. No one is sure how it happened, no one can pinpoint the day when he finally settled in. All we know is that now, two years later, he is implanted in the premises like one of those long-rooted desert trees that sucks up the water for miles around.

Simply to say that Steve *lives* with us is misleading, because that word does not convey the fantastic degree of occupation which he exercises. Stephen Manus, to give him his full name, is no mere inhabitant or tenant of the flat. He is a fixture of it, a presence so constant and unbudging that were the property to be sold he would have to be included in the conveyance, along with the light switches and the radiators. For, like a millionaire recluse or an exquisite endangered salamander, it is only on the rarest occasions that Steve is sighted outside his – correction, outside Pa's – front door. His occupation? Layabout. What he does is nothing, and he goes about it full-time, twenty-four hours a day: Steve rests around the clock. Night or day you'll find him in bed or on the sofa or in an armchair, taking it easy with style and technique. He can stay put for as long as he likes, in any position he chooses. Whereas normal people might grow restless or develop cramp or pins and needles if they didn't move for hours, not so Steve. He's an athlete of immobility.

The funny thing is, you would not guess it to look at him. Like Pa, my first impression of Steve was of an up-and-at– 'em type. 'I like the look of the boy,' Pa had said. 'I like the way he presents himself. He'll go far,' he predicted.

Even to this day, Steve looks like a man with a destination. He stills wears sporty sweaters and ironed cotton shirts with button-down collars, he still has that purposeful, closely shaven jawline. There is no trace of idleness in his appearance; with his healthy red cheeks and his wiry frame, Steve looks like an outdoors man. Only the shoes on his feet – loafers – give any clue to his true nature. But it is only a small clue. After two years' living with him, Steve is still a mystery to me. Every time I think I am making progress, advancing into the district of dreams and fears that make him tick, I hit a brick wall. That's Steve for you: a dead end.

Of course, given the work that I do, there is a hideous irony in my mockery of his sedentary habits.

What an empty phrase: *the work that I do . . .*

It was three years ago that I broke the news of my chosen profession to Pa. I was twenty-three years old.

Pa was stunned. 'What? You're going to *what*?'

I made no reply.

Pa rubbed his face like a man trying to wake up. 'I can't believe what I'm hearing. Johnny, what about your career? Are you just going to let that drop? Stick at it for two more years and you'll be qualified. Just think about it!' Pa urged. 'Two more years and you'll be a chartered accountant!'

I explained to Pa that I had thought about that. 'I'll be fine,' I said. 'It's what I want to do. Don't worry. I'll be all right, you'll see.'

'But how are you going to manage? How are you going to support yourself?' Pa started walking around the room, the way he always did when he became agitated. 'I never heard of anyone making a living in that line of work.' And round he went again, not even looking where he was going – it is a route he has come to know off by heart, that circumnavigation of the two armchairs and the glass coffee-table. 'Where will it take you, this work? What will it lead to?' This was a typical Pa enquiry – Pa, who has always embraced this teleology in respect of employment: that jobs are the cars on the highway of life. 'And, son, I don't want to seem discouraging, but you don't have any training, you don't have any background. Besides,' he said, 'you're all thumbs. Haven't I always told you you've two left hands?' I kept quiet while he shook his head and circled the furniture. 'This is a real shocker for me, Johnny, a real shocker. Frankly, I don't know what to say to you.'

I could not blame him for reacting in this way. Not only had he sunk thousands into my education and training, he had sunk a pile of hope down there, too. My father had been banking on my accountancy career in every way. Thus, for a couple of months, he sought to induce and cajole and beg me to change my mind. One day I had just got out of the bath and was running shivering to my bedroom with a towel around my waist when he approached me in the corridor and said, 'Son, I think it's time we talked about where you are going with your life.'

I kept on running. 'Pa, I've just got out of the bath, OK?'

But Pa was not to be put off and he followed me into my bedroom and addressed me while I towelled my hair and dried my toes and looked for socks. 'Johnny,' he said, 'what do you want from your life? What are your goals?'

I turned from the cupboard to answer but I did not get any further than opening my mouth, because right in front of me my father was holding up a large home-made cardboard lollipop, and on it was written, in arresting black letters, GOALS.

I started laughing.

'Son,' Pa said, 'think about it. You're a man now. What are you aiming for?' He put down the lollipop and brandished another: MONEY. 'Is this what you want? Do you want money?' He pulled out another: FAMILY WITH HOUSE, SECURITY. 'A family, a house?' JOB SATISFACTION, the next placard said. 'How about job satisfaction?' Pa said. 'How important is that to you?' He pointed at my feet. 'Are you really going to wear those socks together? Look, they don't even match.'

'Don't worry,' I said, forcing my damp thighs into some jeans, 'I'm not going out today.'

Pa was about to reply when he remembered the original point of the conversation. With an effort, he raised the three lollipops in his right fist, displaying them in a crooked fan, and then with his left hand he pulled a final lollipop from behind his back: in red letters, EVALUATION AND CHOICE. He stood there for a moment, arms aloft, like a man trying to wave in a wayward aeroplane. 'You've got to work out which of these—' he shook his right hand – 'you want, and why, because I'm telling you now – and believe me, Johnny, I know what I'm talking about, I've been in this world a little longer than you have, listen to what I'm saying to you – I'm telling you that in this line of work you've taken up, you can forget about this—' He dropped the MONEY lollipop on the floor. 'And without money, it becomes very hard to have this—' JOB SATISFACTION fell to the ground. 'And this—' Down with a clatter went the surviving sign, FAMILY WITH HOUSE, SECURITY. 'Take it from me, Johnny, you're running a big, big risk with this – this project of yours.' He wiped sweat from his mouth and waited for me to respond. He had planned this presentation down to the last detail, that was obvious. I envisaged him with his glue and scissors and felt-tips, anxiously cutting circles in the cardboard, rehearsing his speech. Now the decisive moment had arrived: was I going to buy?

To stop Pa from seeing the laugh on my face, I pulled a jumper over my head and pretended to get caught up in the neckhole. 'OK, Pa,' I said, muffling my voice. 'I'll think about it. Thanks very much. I'll get back to you,' I said, still faking a struggle with my jumper.

'I'm glad,' Pa said, his voice trembling a little. 'You think about it. Remember, don't hesitate to come to me with any problems or ideas, or feedback generally. My door is always open,' Pa said.

I am not sure which door my father was referring to when he said that, but of course I never took up his invitation. My mind was made up, and soon after what Pa liked to call our 'meeting' ('Son, have you thought about our meeting? Have you got anything you want to tell me?'), I threw the lollipops into the bin in my bedroom, where they protruded from the yoghurt cartons and the tangerine peel and the other trash. Pa got the message.

Shortly after that, he approached me with his hands in his pockets. I knew what that meant; it meant that he was about to apologize. Whenever Pa is about to say he is sorry, his hands disappear into his trousers.

'Listen, Johnny, I hope I haven't upset you with what I said about your new line of work. I'm sorry if I have.'

'No, Pa, of course you haven't, I said.

He said, 'I just want you to know that I'm on your side, son. I'm right behind you. You do what you want to do. What's important is that you're happy. As long as you're happy, that's all that counts.' In his emotion he left the room and went to the kitchen and put his head into the fridge, pretending to look for something to eat.

What was it, then, that had blown Pa off course like this?

Chairs. That was all. I had decided to make a living making chairs.

'You know, I've been thinking about it,' he said when he returned from the kitchen. 'Maybe it's not such a bad idea.' He started trying to light his pipe, the bowl of which was carved into the wise and unblinking visage of an ancient philosopher.

At that time, Pa was going through a phase of pipe-smoking. 'There's a good market for chairs. People are always going to need to sit down. Let's work it out.' He took a company biro from the row of pens snagged on his breast pocket and flipped open a company scratch pad. 'I'd say that people sit down now more than they ever did. I read about it somewhere – nowadays people are sitting down a whole lot more than they used to.' Pa winked at me with his good eye. 'Which means they're going to need more chairs than ever before.' He breathed on the nib of his biro, then slowly wrote down in capitals – Pa always writes in capitals – MORE CHAIRS THAN EVER BEFORE. 'Yes,' he said, growing excited, 'and when you consider that more people are getting older now and that *old people are always sitting down . . .'* INCREASED DEMAND, Pa wrote.

That clinched it for him. He threw down the biro with a bold finality. 'Increased demand, Johnny. That's what it's all about. They demand, you supply. That's the golden rule.' He stood up, waving his pipe. 'You know, I think you may be on to something. I think you may be on to something big.'

I said carefully, 'I'm not sure how commercial I'm going to be, Pa.'

Pa was sucking away at his pipe, having another attempt at lighting it. 'You may not be sure, son, but I am,' he said, inhaling noisily. The philosopher's cranium released a small cloud. 'I see great possibilities in what you're doing. Which is why I've come to a decision. I'm going to invest in you.'

'Invest?'

'That's right. I'm going to set you up. I'm going to get you a proper workplace with proper equipment. No more scratching around in your bedroom upstairs.'

I stood up in protest. 'There's no need,' I said. 'I'm managing fine as it is. Pa, don't even think about it,' I said.

'This isn't a hand-out, this is business. You'll pay me back with interest once you get going.' He turned towards me with his skewy eyes wide open. 'Johnny, we're going to be partners!'

Looking back at that episode, at my unqualmish acceptance of finance, I cannot avoid a feeling of shame. In those days I found my father's donations a marvellously uncomplicated business. I needed the money, and not just for tools, materials and workspace – the fact was, I needed the money generally. I was twenty-three – I needed to live, didn't I? And as I saw it, money was simply part of the deal with Pa: subsidies, allowances and disbursements came with the terrain of his acquaintance. Besides, in the final analysis I was doing him a favour by taking his money – what else was he going to spend it on? Why shouldn't he buy a flat for his kids if that was what made him happy?

Maybe *buy*, with its connotation of outright purchase, is not quite the right word, because that makes it sound as though Pa just reached into his pocket and handed over the cash. It did not happen that way. To finance the transaction, Pa had to remortgage his house, the family home at 75 Turtledove Lane. The agreement was that Rosie and I would pay what rent we could afford. Property was buoyant, Pa said. You'll see, he told us happily as he showed us his name on the deeds, we're going to come out of this smelling of roses.

Soon after Pa bought the flat the property market plunged. For two years now we have kept watch on the house prices, waiting for an end to their descent like spectators waiting for the jerking bloom of a skydiver's parachute as he plummets towards the earth. But two years on, the prices are still falling and interest rates are still rising and Pa has to make whacking monthly payments which he cannot afford to make. Even so, he has never asked Rosie or me for a cent, with the result that no real rent has ever been paid. Now, there are reasons for this inexcusable situation. In my case, the answer is poverty: I'm broke. Unlike two years ago, though, at least now I experience genuine guilt about it. But by the operation of a circuitous, morally paralysing causality, somehow this guilt expiates its cause: the worse I feel about not paying Pa, the more penalized and thus virtuous and thus better I feel. As for Rosie – well, Rosie has other things to do with her money and no one, least of all Pa, is going to give her a hard time about that. Allowances have to be made as far as Rosie is concerned because allowances have always been made as far as Rosie is concerned. Besides, there is Steve. There is no point in being unrealistic about it – Steve is not the type to pay for anything. Steve lives for free.

And yet, despite all of this, Rosie sticks with him. It is hard to understand, to identify the perverse adherent at work between them. Rosie has wit, intelligence and beauty, and all of the Breezes have had a special soft spot for her for as long as anybody can remember. She has dark eyes set widely apart and a mane of auburn hair which ran until recently down her back like a fire. She is twenty-eight, two years older than me, and by any reasonable standard Steve Manus, agreeable though he is in his own way, is not fit to lick her boots. Rosie herself recognizes this, and although Steve shares her bed and her earnings, for some months now she has denied that he is her boyfriend.

'It's finished,' she says. 'You don't think I'd stay with a creep like that, do you?'

But – but what about their cohabitation?

Rosie reads the question on my face. 'He's out of here,' she says, 'as soon as he finds somewhere to live. I'm not having that parasite in this house for one minute longer than I have to.' We are in the kitchen. She raises her voice so that Steve, who is in the sitting-room, can hear her. 'If the Slug doesn't find a place by this time next month, that's it, I'm kicking it out,' she shouts. 'Let it slime around on someone else's floor for a change!'

Then the same thing always happens. Rosie goes away for two or three weeks to the other side of the world – Kuala Lumpur, Tokyo, Chicago – and by the time she descends from the skies we are back to square one. Square one is not a pleasant place to be. It is bad enough having Steve in the house, but when both he and my sister are here together for any length of time – usually when she has a spell of short-haul work – things become sticky.

It starts when Rosie comes home exhausted in the evening, still wearing her green and blue stewardess's uniform. Instead of putting her feet up, she immediately spends an hour cleaning. 'Look at this mess, just look at this pigsty,' she says, furiously gathering things up – Steve's things, invariably, because although fastidious about his personal appearance, he is just about the messiest and most disorderly person I know. On Rosie goes, rearranging cushions and snatching at newspapers. 'Whose shoes are these? What about this plate – whose is that?' Steve and I keep quiet, even if she is binning perfectly usable objects, because the big danger when Rosie comes home and starts picking things up is that she will hurl something at you. (Oh, yes, make no mistake, Rosie can be violent. In those split seconds of temper she will pick up the nearest object to hand and aim that missile between your eyes with a deadly seriousness. If she's not careful, some day she will do somebody a real injury.) Rosie does not rest until she has filled and knotted a bin-liner and until she has hoovered the floors and scrubbed the sinks. She sticks to this routine even if the flat is already clean on her return. She puffs up the sofa, complains bitterly that the sink is filthy and redoes the washing up, which she claims has been badly done. ('The glasses!' she cries, holding aloft an example. 'How many times do I have to tell you to dry the glasses *by hand*!') Only once all of the objects in the sitting-room – many of which have remained untouched since they were moved by her the day before – have been fractionally repositioned does she finally relent. But what then? This is what concerns me, the horrified question I see expressed on my sister's face once she has finished. What happens once everything is in its place?

Usually what happens next is that Steve gets it in the neck.

'What have you done today?' she demands.

'Well,' Steve says, 'I've . . .'

'You haven't done anything, have you?'

The poor fellow opens his mouth to speak, then closes it again.

'You're pathetic,' Rosie says quietly. 'Don't talk to me. Your voice revolts me.' Then she lights a cigarette and momentarily faces the television, her legs crossed. She is still wearing her uniform. She inhales; the tip of her cigarette glitters. She turns around and looks Steve in the eye. 'Well?' Steve does not know what to say. Rosie turns away in disgust. 'As I thought. Slug is too spineless to speak. *Pathetic*.'

'I . . . No,' Steve says bravely, 'I'm not.'

Suddenly Rosie bursts into laughter. 'No?' She looks at him with amusement. 'You're not pathetic?'

'No,' Steve says with a small, uncertain smile.

'Oh, you sweetie,' Rosie says, sliding along the sofa towards him. Holding him and speaking in a baby voice, she says, 'You don't do anything, do you, honey bear? You just sit around all day and make a mess like a baby animal, don't you, my sweet?'

Steve nods, happy with the swing of her mood, and nestles like a child in her arms. With luck, Rosie, who can be such good value when she is happy, has found respite from the awful, intransigent spooks that have somehow fastened on her, and we can all relax and get on with our evening.

How, then, do I put up with such horrible scenes? The answer is, by treating them as such: as scenes. It's the only way. If I took their dramas to heart – if I let them come anywhere near my heart – I'd finish up like my father.

3

I have poured myself a glass of water. This waiting around is thirsty work, especially if, like me, you're already dehydrated by a couple of lunchtime drinks. These came immediately after the refereeing débâcle, when Pa and I walked over to the nearest bar for a beer. Afterwards, the plan was, we were off back to Pa's place to watch a proper game of football on the television: the relegation decider between Rockport United and Ballybrew. We Breezes, of course, follow United.

It was only when Pa returned with the drinks and took off his glasses to wipe the mud from them that I was able to observe his face closely. I thought, Jesus Christ.

It was his eyes. Looked at closely in the midday light, they were appalling. The eyeballs – I gasped when I saw the eyeballs: tiny red beads buried deep in violet pouches that sagged like emptied, distended old purses. Pa had always had troublesome old eyes, but now, I suddenly saw, things had gone a stage further. These were black eyes, the kind you got from punches; these were bona fide shiners.

How was this possible? How could this assault have happened?

I am afraid that the answer was painfully obvious. It was plain as pie that Pa has walked into every punch that life had swung in his direction. With his whole, undefensive heart, Pa has no guard. Every time a calamity has rolled along, there he has been to collect it right between his poor, crooked peepers. And in the last three days, of course, two real haymakers had made contact: first, the news that his job was in jeopardy; and second, Merv. It was doubtful that Pa had slept at all since Thursday night, the night of the crash.

I remembered the time I became acquainted with Merv: about four years ago, when I was looking for my first job and needed a suit for interviews. Pa said he had the answer to my problem. 'There's this fellow in my office with a terrible curvature of the spine,' he said, 'but you'd hardly know it to look at him. He strolls around like a guardsman. It's his suits that make all the difference,' Pa said. 'The jackets fit him like gloves. There's the man you want – the man who makes his suits.'

That was Merv – not the tailor, but the dapper hunchback. Every time I've met him I have been unable, hard as I might try, to keep my eyes off his back, off the hump, under his shirt.

Pa took a slug of his beer and threw me a packet of salt and vinegar crisps. Then he opened a packet of his own.

We sat there in silence for a few moments, crunching the potatoes. I said, 'Are you sure you're OK? You're not looking well.' He did not reply. I drank some beer and regarded him again. Then I said, 'Listen, Pa. I know you don't agree with me on this, but I really think you ought to consider packing in the reffing.' Pa tilted his face towards the ceiling and tipped the last crumbs from the crisp packet into his mouth. 'I'm not saying you should just sit at home doing nothing,' I said. 'Do something else. I don't know, take up squash or something.' No, that was too dangerous: I could just see him stretched out on the floor of the court, soaked in sweat and clutching his heart. 'Or golf,' I said. 'Golf is a great game. Just give up the reffing. It isn't worth it, Pa. You don't get any thanks for what you do.'

Pa took a mouthful of beer and shook his head. 'Johnny, I can't. If I wasn't there, who else would do it? Those kids rely on me. They're counting on me to be there. Besides,' he said, 'I want to put something back into the game. Pay my dues.'

This last reason, especially, I did not and do not understand. The fact of the matter is that Pa, never having played the game, has not received anything from it which he could possibly pay back. Pa owes soccer nothing.

It was only thanks to me that he came into contact with football in the first place. I was eight years old and had begun to take part in Saturday morning friendlies in the park, and, along with the other parents, Pa took to patrolling the touch-line in his dark sheepskin coat. 'Go on, Johnny!' he used to shout as he ran up and down. 'Go on, son!' At first, my father was just like the other fathers, an ordinary spectator. But there came a day when he showed up in a track suit, the blue track suit he wears to this day with the old-fashioned stripes running down the legs. When, at half-time, he called the team together and the boys found themselves listening to his exhortations and advice, it dawned on them that Mr Breeze – a man who had never scored a goal in his life – had appointed himself coach. While Pa's pep talks lacked tactical shrewdness, they were full of encouragement. 'Never say die, men,' he urged as we chewed the bitter chunks of lemon he handed out. 'We're playing well. We can pull back the four goals we need. Billy,' he said, taking aside our tiny, untalented goalkeeper, 'you're having a blinder. Don't worry about those two mistakes. It happens to the best of us. Keep it up, Sean,' Pa said to our least able outfield player. 'Don't forget, you're our midfield general.'

Pa's involvement did not end there. No, pretty soon he had come up with a car pool, a team strip (green and white) and, without originality, a name: the Rovers. He organized a mini-league, golden-boot competitions, man-of-the-match awards, knock-out tournaments and, finally, he began refereeing games. He was terrible at it right from the start. Never having been a player himself, he had no idea what was going on. Offside, obstruction, handball, foul throw – Pa knew the theory of these offences but had no ability to detect them in practice. This incompetence showed, and mattered, even at the junior level of the Rovers' matches between nine- and ten-year-olds. Needless to say, it was not much fun being the ref's son. It made me an outsider in my own side.

I looked at my father, Eugene Breeze, sitting in front of me with his pint, resting. The creased, criss-crossed face, the leaking blue venation under the skin, the thin white hair pasted by sweat against the forehead. The red eyes blinking like hazard lights.

'Pa,' I said as gently as I could. 'Face it. It's time to quit. It's time to move on to something else.'

He shrugged obstinately. 'I'm not a quitter,' he said.

That was true – he's not a man to throw in the towel. When I stopped playing for the team – I must have been about eleven years old – Pa kept going. He kept right on refereeing the

Rovers, running around the park every Saturday morning waist-deep in a swarm of youngsters. Even when the Rovers eventually disbanded, he did not give up. On the contrary, he decided to enter the refereeing profession properly. He bought himself a black outfit, boots with a bolt of lightning flashing from the ankle to the toe, red and yellow cards, a waterproof notebook and the Association Football rule book. Then one day he came home with a flushed face and a paper furled up in a pink ribbon. Wordlessly he handed me the scroll. I opened it and there it was in bold, splendid ink, *Eugene Breeze*, spectacularly printed in a large Gothic script.

This is to certify that Eugene Breeze is a Class E referee, the document announced. It was signed by Matthew P. Brett, Secretary of the Football Association.

'Congratulations,' I said. I was sixteen and laconic.

'I took the exams and passed them straight off,' Pa said. He retrieved the certificate from me and slapped it against his palm. 'Do you realize, Johnny,' he said, 'do you realize that now I'm *qualified*?'

'Great,' I said. 'You're in the way,' I said, leaning sideways to see the television.

'This could lead anywhere.' He shook the certificate as though it were a magical document of discovery and empowerment, a passport, blank cheque and round-the-world ticket rolled into one. 'Who knows, with a bit of luck I could be refereeing professionally in a couple of years' time, couldn't I, Johnny? I mean, I know it sounds crazy, but it's *possible*, isn't it?'

That's right, I said. It's possible.

Possibilities! Pa, the numbskull, is a great one for possibilities. Stars in his eyes, he signed up officially with the Football Association and put his name down on the match list. He developed a scrupulous pre-match routine, ticking off checklists, boning up on the laws of the game and the weather reports, checking his studs and, late on the night before, ironing his kit and laying it out on the floor like a flat black ghost. But his dream of ascending the refereeing ladder did not materialize. For a while he took charge of good fixtures, games between ambitious young teenagers playing for serious clubs.

But then, after his lack of ability became known and complaints had been made, the invitations dried up. 'Never mind,' he said to me eventually. 'I'll find my own level.' That was when he took to wandering around football fields in his kit, haunting the touchlines, his silver whistle suspended unquietly from his neck. He would approach teams that were warming up and say, 'Need a ref? Look, I'm qualified . . .' and he would unfurl his certificate. Usually that was enough to do the trick, and that is how Pa has ended up where he is, officiating bad-tempered confrontations between pub teams and office XIs, ridiculed and bad-mouthed by players and onlookers alike. Even when he does well the abuse keeps coming, because the referee – that instrument of injustice – is never right. And still he persists and still, rain or shine, every weekend finds him out on the heath, looking for a game.

This state of affairs is unlikely to last for long, because Pa has become truly notorious for his incapability, even amongst occasional teams. One time he so mishandled a game that the players, unanimous in their infuriation, ordered him to leave the field; and so Pa is famous, in the small world of Rockport amateur football, for being the only referee ever to have been sent off. As a result, he is finding it harder and harder to get a game. Increasingly his polite offers of his services draw a blank and he has to content himself with running the line, waving the offsides with his red handkerchief. The day cannot be far away when my father finds that, like it or not, his officiating days are behind him.

'And how about you?' Pa asked, dropping two fresh beers on the table. 'How's it going? How's the exhibition coming along?'

'Just fine,' I said, raising my glass to my mouth. 'It's all under control.'

The exhibition. Two weeks tomorrow, on 16 May, my chairs are scheduled to go on show at the Simon Devonshire Gallery. It took months of pleading, telephoning, writing, lying, boasting and begging to get that show. The good news finally came one day last October, when Simon Devonshire rang me in person. 'Well, John,' he said, 'you can't keep a good man down. A week starting from 16 May, next year, how does that sound to you?'

I could not believe it. Simon Devonshire himself, patron, connoisseur and big shot, was giving me the nod. This was it, this was the big break. 'Are you serious?' I said with a laugh.

'Certainly I'm serious,' Devonshire said. 'Now, you're not going to let me down, are you, John? I'm putting my neck on the line for you. You appreciate that, don't you?'

'Of course,' I said breathlessly, 'of course. Don't worry, Mr Devonshire,' I said. 'You won't regret this.'

I was overjoyed. I rang Angela straight away. She was overjoyed, too. 'Johnny, that's marvellous!' She burst out laughing. Her laugh: a wonder, a full, chuckling letting go, a pure unzipping of joy . . . What a find Angela was. To this day I cannot believe my luck. You hear stories of those poor boys who, steering their goats from thistle to thistle upon some African tableland, happen upon a priceless stone in the dust. Well, that was how it was with me and Angela. It was during my time as a trainee accountant, when I was doing an audit in the offices of a transportation company out in some small wet town in the middle of nowhere. It was my job to make sure that the books balanced, that the debits and credits added up, a lonely, discouraging job, the nights spent on my own in a two-star hotel, the days working away in the small isolated room to which I had been consigned, a hole darkened from wall to wall with piles of thick, inscrutable ledgers – auditors always get the lousiest workspace going. After about a week, the task arrived of checking up on three trucks that the company had listed amongst its assets. It was time to pay a visit to the warehouse.

It was raining. I walked quickly across the muddy car-park to the Portakabin that served as the warehouse office and introduced myself to the girl who was writing there, her head lowered over her paper. Hello, I said, I'm with the auditors. If it's possible, I'd like to do a stock-check and . . . I did not say another word, because suddenly I found myself looking into these two blue rocks.

'Of course,' the girl said, brushing her hair from her face, smiling. 'Just go straight in.' Then she looked at me and laughed, and even now it thrills me to recall that sound and the sight of her head thrown back dramatically, the paper-white teeth shining in her open mouth, the red tongue clean as a cat's.

Pa pushed his beer aside, licked the froth from his upper lip and said, 'Johnny, I've been thinking. There's a lot of people with back trouble in this world. A lot of people need chairs they can sit on without hurting the base of the spine. I'm telling you, you should hear the complaints I get from the people at work. It's a complicated thing, the spine. A mystery. Even doctors don't know how it works. Anyway, I was thinking that there must be a market for specially designed chairs for people with back problems. Do you follow me?' Pa spread his pale, veiny hands on the table. 'I reckon that if you could come up with something along those lines you'd be made. I read something about it the other day,' he said. 'In the paper. They've now got chairs with no backs. You just have a seat which is tilted forwards and these pads to rest your knees on. Did you know that?'

'It's not a bad idea, Pa,' I said, but I left it at that. In the furniture circles that I move in, it is artistic and not ergonomic considerations that prevail. The people who go to Simon Devonshire's are not interested in lumbar comfort. They want pieces that make a statement, that provoke discussion. They want chairs with suggestive titles. Take last year's two successes. The first was a chair called *ouch*. On its back were carved figures engaged in all kinds of monsterish copulations: goats doing it with men, women doing it with horses, dogs doing it with cats and so forth. But they were not the main feature; that was the wooden phallus which rose from the middle of the seat, so located that you could not sit on the chair without being penetrated by it. But that, of course, was not a problem, since the chair was not designed to be sat on. The same thing applied to the second success of the season. Entitled *Caramba, Yes*, it was just an ordinary wooden chair with four legs and a back, a chair of the cheap, plain, functional kind that you saw in garden sheds all over the country. Because of its strong ironical content, it is cheaper to buy certain new cars than *Caramba, Yes*.

Devonshire signed me for an exhibition on the strength of

one piece which he displayed and immediately sold: the love chair, which consisted of two ash seats with splayed legs connected by a mutual arm. Calling the piece the love chair was Devonshire's idea, not mine, but I was happy to go along with his suggestion – what could be wrong with love? Pa's favourite work of mine, though, is the pew, a kneeling-stool attached to a small desk where the supplicant might rest the elbows: a prie-dieu. I finished it about eight months ago and to my surprise he expressed a liking for it.

'I like it,' he said. 'I really do. I think it's the best thing you've done.' He circled it slowly, examining it. 'I could use a chair like this,' he said. 'I could use it when I say my prayers.'

I smiled. I was pleased that someone like Pa, who actually prayed to God, saw practical value in the chair. I was surprised, too. I had not foreseen that someone might appreciate the object so literally.

'I could put it in the spare bedroom upstairs,' Pa said. 'I could go up there when I needed some peace and quiet, some time for myself.'

Pa could not have the pew, though, because I had promised it to Angela as a gift. There it is over there, next to the fireplace. She uses it as a platform for her plants. It does not look particularly good that way, obscured by the fern, but it's hers now, and if that's what she wants to do with it, that's fine by me. That's the great thing about Angela: everything she does is fine by me.

'Well, anyway,' Pa said, lifting his glass, 'here's to the exhibition. You've earned it, son. You've worked hard and you've gotten what you've deserved.'

I returned the gesture with a hollow smile. I did not say anything to Pa about the exhibition because I did not want to upset him, not now. I'd wait a while. I'd wait till things started looking up for him.

Things looking up: how was I supposed to know what was going to happen?

4

Let me say this: Angela's place is not an easy place to cool your heels. This is a studio apartment. Aside from a small bathroom and a kitchen, there is only one room – the living/bedroom, which as a place of entertainment is a dead loss. The television is broken, I have read the books and heard all the records. The kitchen is no better: the bread is stale, the cupboards are empty and there's nothing in the fridge. Usually you can count on finding some ruby orange juice or a tub of pasta salad from the delicatessen, but not tonight. There isn't even any milk. You'd think that Steve had dropped in.

Angela must be pretty busy at work to allow things to get this way. They really drive her hard at Bear Elias, and if she does not go into the office at the weekend it is only because she has brought work home. When she gets back in the evenings, the first thing she does is head straight for the sofa and bed down for an hour. Only then, when I have brought her a cup of tea and rubbed her feet and warmed her toes, does she have the energy to talk. And, as if her job were not demanding enough, she has taken to going to the gym. At least three evenings a week she works out at the local fitness club, courtesy of her corporate membership. I'm not complaining, she has never looked better. But just lately arranging to see her has almost become a question of booking an appointment.

She is now forty-five minutes late.

There will be a perfectly reasonable explanation for her absence. As occurs in a million appointments every day, an innocent delay has arisen. She is late, and that is all there is to it.

For the sake of variety, I climb up to the bed – climb, because the bed is a king-sized bunk which hangs from the high ceiling on big white-painted chains. When Angela first moved here, three years ago, she and I had a private sentimental nickname for this loft: the love-nest, we used to call it.

I lie down on my back with closed eyes. I breathe deeply.

There is so much room up here that three people could stretch out in comfort. In fact, it took Angela and me a little time to become accustomed to the space. In the year before she moved in here – our first year together – when I was living at home with Pa, we did our sleeping together at her old place, a cheap flat by the docks. Angela had a single bed, one as narrow as a train berth, and when the underground passed below and sent vibrations through the house, the two of us lay there rocking like journeyers on an overnight express. Who is to say that the sensation of travel was not an appropriate one? After all, we were going places. I was about to embark on my chair-making venture and Angela had just started her MBA, and like motorists entranced and quickened by new cities tantalizingly pledged on highway signboards, during those shaking nights our quickly looming futures kept us awake for hours, talking, talking. Fired up, emboldened by the rich proximity of our goals, we travelled easily through the hours of darkness, all the while wrapped up together like a package, our legs intertwined, our arms locked into bear hugs. We hung on like this all night. We had to – the bed was so small that we couldn't roll over without falling out.

I open my eyes. Jesus, I hope she's all right. I hope nothing's happened to her.

I rise with a start and climb down the ladder. I'm damned if I am going to worry. The chances of Angela not safely returning home must be at least a million to one. Only a professional nail-biter like Pa would get worked up by those kinds of odds.

But if I were him, I would be fearful of long shots, too.

The incident in the pub this morning. Now that's what I call a dark horse.

Pa and I had just sucked down the remains of our beers and were about to make a move when, pushing through the crush, a man suddenly came forward and pointed at Pa. 'I know you,' he said. He kept pointing. 'It's Breeze, isn't it? You're him. You're Gene Breeze, aren't you?'

Pa glanced at me nervously and said, 'Yes, as a matter of fact I am.' He turned to the man. 'How – how can I help you?'

'I thought I recognized you,' the man said. 'I said to myself, I know that face from somewhere.'

It is important, here, to point something out: the most remarkable thing about the newcomer was his size. He was a midget. He could not have been more than four feet tall.

I picked up my coat and said, 'Let's go, Pa.'

The man said, 'You want to know if I've got any problems, Breeze? You want to know if I've got any complaints? Well, pal, I do. I've got a whole pile of fucking complaints.'

He put his beer down and stood at the end of the table. Pa was cornered.

Pa said, 'How can I help you, Mr . . . '

'Don't worry about my name, Breeze, you're the one with questions to answer.' Again he jabbed his index finger in Pa's direction. 'You got that, Breeze? *You're* the one doing the answering around here.'

I could not believe it. This runt, this *titch*, was threatening two fully grown men.

'How is it,' the man demanded, 'that I'm late for work almost every day of the week? Eh, Breeze? How is it that I spend two grand a year on fucking travel and still I get to stand in a crowded, dirty train every morning – if I'm lucky?' He wiped the small wet hole of his mouth and started moving towards Pa. 'Well? I only live fifteen miles from Rockport: so why does it take me, on average, one hour to get into town?'

Pa, his face yellow-grey again, was completely lost. He started shrinking into his anorak as the stranger slowly advanced like a miniature gunman, punctuating his sentences with absurd stomps of his cowboy boots. The stranger said, 'You haven't got much to say for yourself, have you, Breeze? Eh? Why do I spend half my life freezing on a fucking train platform? Well, Breeze? Sorry – well, *Gene*?'

'I . . .' Pa said. 'I . . .'

I decided to intervene. 'That's enough,' I said. 'Listen, I don't know who you are, but . . .'

'Enjoying yourself, Breeze?' the man sneered. 'Having fun, are you? I am. I should do this more often. I should *liaise* with you more often.' Now the midget's red face, bright as a stop light, was directly below Pa's. 'I tell you what,' he said. 'You want to know how I feel, Gene, old boy? You really want to know how I feel?'

The man spat straight into Pa's face, the saliva spurting up and sticking with a tacky splash on his eyebrow and on the frame of his glasses.

The man drew back. 'There you go, Gene. Stick that in your report.' Then, before I could react, before I could snap his fucking dwarf's neck, he walked off.

'Pa,' I said. 'Pa, Jesus, I . . .'

Pa had not moved. He was still frozen in the corner with shock, the spittle now slowly dripping down on to his lips.

I took out his red linesman's handkerchief and wiped his face and glasses. 'Come on,' I said, stuffing the handkerchief back into his pocket. 'Let's get out of here.'

That fleck of shit spat at Pa because Pa is the manager of the Rockport Railway Network, Northern Section. He is the man responsible for the smooth running of two hundred and sixty trains a day. It's a large responsibility which has not been lessened, it has to be said, by the poster campaign which the Network has recently embarked on. Plastered over every train and every train station in north Rockport is a photograph of my father holding a telephone. It is not a very good photograph: his hair is uncombed, his cream tie clashes with his brown shirt and grey jacket and, worst of all, his face bears an apprehensive and culpable expression. The caption reads:

GENE BREEZE – AT YOUR SERVICE

Hello, I'm Gene Breeze, your Network Manager. If you have any comments – good or bad – about the service we provide, let me know. I want to know how you feel to help me meet your requirements. So don't hold back. Liaise with me or my staff on Rockport 232597.

THE ROCKPORT NETWORK – WE'RE GETTING THERE

The network motto, 'We're getting there', has, of course, become something of a joke, because everybody knows that the Network is getting nowhere. It has personnel problems, rolling-stock problems, signalling problems and investment problems. Above all, it has delay problems – delays that have been attributed to such malign agents of nature as swans (flying into the overhead lines), leaves (falling on the tracks) and rodents (gnawing into cables). Staff morale is low and passenger dissatisfaction is high, and for an hour at the end of every day Pa has to listen to the abuse and anger of the Network users. That is on top of the nine hours he puts in trying to run the railroad itself.

It angers me to think of what he goes through. Not long ago, I tried to talk him out of fielding the complaints personally.

'I have to, son,' he said. 'I have to. I owe it to the customers. It's not right that I invite them to ring me without me being there at least some of the time. They are my clients. They have a right to talk to me.'

'But, Pa, you have a public relations team to look after that. Let them answer the calls.'

'As the manager,' Pa said, 'I am responsible for the complaints. The buck stops with me,' he said. 'The way I see it, being answerable to the public means just that: answering the public.'

'But the other network managers don't do that,' I said. 'Pa, you're the only one who actually does what those posters say.'

'You're right,' Pa admitted. 'But then, it wasn't their idea to start this campaign.'

I said, 'It was your idea?'

'Yes,' he said proudly. 'I was the one who suggested it to the directors. No matter what Paddy Browne says, I'm not devoid of ideas.'

Paddy Browne is the Network Secretary and, according to Pa, the man behind the moves to depose him. It was Paddy Browne who recently suggested to Pa that he should think of early retirement. That day, Pa came round to the flat and stood fuming in my basement workshop as I tinkered, for the sake of appearances, with a piece of wood.

'Early retirement? Early retirement? You know what that means, don't you? It means the sack, that's what it means.' He started wandering around the room, weaving his way between the various obstacles. He uttered the loathsome name once more: 'Paddy Browne.' He pointed at the door. 'He wants me out, that's what he wants. No, no, I can see it with my own eyes,' Pa said, waving me down as though I had voiced a protest. 'He undermines everything I do. Every time I say anything at a meeting, Paddy's there with a "Yes, but", and "Surely what you're trying to say is this . . ." It's eating away at me, Johnny, it's tearing me apart. Johnny,' Pa said wildly, 'Johnny, he's after my blood. He won't rest until he sees me out.'

'Are you sure you're not reading too much into it?' I said.

'Listen, the man has commissioned a study of the management structure, he's bringing in people from the outside. The management structure! That's a good one! The management structure is *me*: I'm the management structure!'

I said nothing.

Pa said, 'And I know what they're going to recommend. They're going to recommend my dismissal.'

'You don't know that, Pa,' I said.

'Just you wait and see,' he said. 'I know how Browne operates. He's going to produce these bar charts and efficiency graphs which will show that I've got to go. Johnny, you should see the stuff he comes up with. It's all green arrows and red arrows and flow charts and diagrams. He goes around with this portable computer, this lap-top, as he calls it, and everything he writes comes out looking like – like the Ten Commandments.' Pa suddenly raised his voice. 'You don't believe me? Here,' he said, stormily snatching a folder from his briefcase and flying sheets of paper into the air, 'here, read this. Just read it.'

I took the folder and flicked through its contents, a twenty-page company report of some kind. The document, headlines printed in bold, key points emphasized in italics and statistics illustrated by multicoloured pie charts, was immaculate. The sentences were short and unambiguous and the concluding opinion was headed 'Findings', as though unimpeachable discoveries of fact had been made. I handed the papers back to Pa. 'I see what you mean,' I said.

'What did I tell you? I'm right, aren't I?' Pa closed his briefcase. 'I haven't got a hope against that kind of presentation,' he said. 'Not a hope. Hell's bells, Johnny, all I know about is trains.'

I said cautiously, 'Maybe retirement wouldn't be such a bad

thing. Think of all the free time you'd have. Think of all the things you could do.'

Pa swung around. 'Free time? Are you crazy? I don't want free time! I want to work! Besides,' he said in a different voice, 'I'll be honest with you, we need the money. If I retired, who would make the mortgage payments on this flat?'

'Pa, sell the flat. Rosie and me'll be fine. Don't let us stop you.'

Pa said, 'We were unlucky with this place. As soon as we bought it the market fell. They say prices never dropped so quickly in twenty years.' He shook his head. 'We can't afford to sell now. We'd lose too much.'

Although Pa was telling the truth about the property market, I knew that he was just using it as an excuse. The fact of the matter is, Pa will never sell the flat so long as Rosie and I are still in need of it.

So there is something else for me not to worry about – the calamitous possibility of Pa being laid off tomorrow, the day that the management report comes out. Calamitous is not an exaggeration. My father without employment is simply unimaginable. His veneration of work is such that, whenever he picks up a newspaper, the first place he turns to, before even the sports pages, are the appointments pages.

'Listen to this, son,' he says, reading out an advertisement in a low, reverential voice. 'And this,' he says turning to another one, 'just listen to this one.' He holds up the sheets to the light in wonderment. 'Would you believe it?' he says. 'Would you believe it?'

There he sits, his mouth open. And we are not concerned with especially desirable posts here, with company directorships or academic sinecures. No, we are concerned with ordinary vacancies, openings for sales engineers and area housing managers, for biomedical technicians and senior improvements officers. These are the jobs that enthral Pa.

It is almost inevitable, when he peruses the jobs pages, that he suddenly drops the paper, produces a pair of scissors and starts cutting away at the broadsheet. 'Johnny,' he says as he snips away, 'Johnny, this is it. This is the one.' He thrusts his handiwork at me and sits back to study my reaction.

SALES PEOPLE – *Young progressive advertising company requires Sales People in all areas to carry out major expansion programme. Training and support will be provided, car with a telephone a pre-requisite. Generous expense allowance plus commission.*

'Well? What do you think?'

'Pa, Steve doesn't have a car.'

He is thrown for a moment, but then he bounces right back. 'That's just a detail,' he says boldly. 'What's a car? We can find Steve a car no problem. No,' he says, waving the cutting like a winning lottery ticket, 'this is just the job for Stephen. Look – it says he'll get training and support. I'm telling you, that boy has it in him to do great things. It's not too late. He's just a young man, he has his whole life ahead of him. With a bit of help, who knows how far he'll go?' Pa tucks the cutting into his wallet. 'I'll send it to him straight away.'

I have been through this with my father many times before, so I do not say anything. The short point is that Steve is not a worker. He has not lifted a finger in the five years that I have known him and he is not about to change now. While his inner being may be a mystery, I do know Steve this well: if you offered him a salary of twenty thousand a month to do exactly what he liked, he would turn you down – it would sound too much like work. I have not reached this conclusion lightly. Like Pa, I used to pass on to Steve ads which I had seen in the newspapers. That's right. I used to get the scissors out, too. Whenever I got wind of a cushy number, old Steve was the first to hear about it. But that strategy was like Steve himself: it didn't work; and after what happened last time, I have sworn that I will never try it again.

Wanted, the advertisement said. *Trustworthy house-sitter for period residence while owners go abroad for a month. Generous pay.*

'Steve,' I said, 'take a look at that. Now that's what I call a job.'

Steve reached out from the sofa and looked at the newspaper for a whole minute. 'Thanks, Johnny,' he said. Then he carefully placed the paper on the floor.

I made a decision. I fetched a sheet of paper and typed out the application myself. 'Sign here,' I said to Steve.

'God, thanks, John,' Steve said as he wrote his name.

Then I posted the letter. I went to the post office, bought a stamp and personally mailed the fucker.

The reply came quickly. It was good news: Steve had been granted an interview on Thursday, at nine in the morning. Great, Steve said. Great stuff.

That Thursday morning I arose early – those were the days when I was still productive, back in September of last year. By eight-fifteen, though, Steve had not stirred from his bed: Rosie's bed: the bed which Pa had shelled out for. When I opened the bedroom door, there he was, a mound under the duvet.

'Wake up, Steve,' I said, shaking him by the shoulder. 'Wake up. You've got to go to your interview.'

He rolled over and stared at me with uncomprehending, unconscious eyes. Then he rolled over again and went back to sleep. There was nothing I could do to rouse him. I said to Rosie, Rosie, for God's sake, tell him to get up. Tell him to go.

Rosie, who was busy getting ready for work, said, 'Oh, forget it. He won't do it, he's useless.' She put her head through the door and shouted, 'You're useless, aren't you, Slug?' Then suddenly she snatched up a handful of objects – lipsticks, hairbrushes, books – and started hurling them at him. 'You just lie there and rot and vegetate and do nothing, you bastard! Get up!' she screamed, tugging at the duvet. 'Get up, you shit!'

'Take it easy, Rosie,' I said. 'It's all right, don't worry about it.'

Rosie started weeping with anger and humiliation, the tears leaving tracks through her deep stewardess's make-up. 'He's so . . . He's just so . . .'

I said, 'It's OK, Rosie . . . Rosie, it's all right.' I led her out of the bedroom and up to the front door. 'We'll sort it out. Now you just go to work, all right?'

'He's such a bastard, Johnny,' Rosie said, swallowing back mucus and cleaning her face. 'He's such a bastard.' Then she put on her green hat and headed out into the street to the job she hates.

What a dope I was to allow myself to get into that situation – to allow myself to get involved with Steve like that.

Never again.

Pa, though, does not see it that way. Again and again is his motto. As far as he is concerned, where there is life there is hope, and in spite of everything he still believes that inside Steve there lie secret deposits of energy waiting to be tapped, gushers. Pa has got it wrong. Steve is not the North Sea or the Arabian peninsula. There are no oilfields in Steve.

5

I have to be careful – careful of letting myself be sucked in by Rosie and Steve and their wretched problems which I can do nothing about. But I can't stop it because I have to live with them; and I have to live with them because there's nowhere else for me to go.

This may sound strange, but not long ago I believed that I *had* gone, that I had swum free from the dismal whirlpool of their lives and had hauled up here, with Angela. My clothes were in that cupboard, my toothbrush and razor were in that bathroom cabinet and my books and records were stacked on those shelves over there, indistinguishable from Angela's. I spent nine nights out of ten here and the only reason I ever went back to the Breeze flat was because that's where my studio was, in the basement. As far as I was concerned, I had flown the cage.

Then one day – this was about four months ago, in January – an electoral registration form arrived in the mail. I got out a biro and filled in the form. I wrote our names, Angela Flanagan and John Breeze, in the Names of Occupants box.

Angela laughed when she picked up the form that evening. 'What's this?' She pointed at my name, then started laughing again.

I didn't see what was so funny.

She came over and sat down next to me. She put an arm around my shoulders and gave me a soft, sympathetic kiss on the cheek, and then another. There was a silence as she continued to hold me close to her, her face brushing against mine, her light breath exhaled in sweet gusts. 'Oh, Johnny,' she said. I kept still, waiting for the retraction of that laughter, confirmation that this place was officially my home. It never came. She released me, kissed me one more time and went over to the table. She picked up a yellow highlighter, opened a fat ring binder and started reading, brightening the text with crisp stripes.

Ring binders. I'm sick of the sight of them. Towards the end of January, a messenger arrived with ten cardboard boxloads of the things – heavy, glossy purple files stamped with the Bear Elias logo.

'It's the Telecom privatization,' Angela said excitedly as she tore the tape from the boxes. 'There are over ten thousand documents. I've got to store them here because there simply isn't the space in the office.'

'Where are you going to put them? There's no storage space here either.'

She ripped open a box, the sellotape tearing crudely away from the cardboard. 'I thought that I might be able to use the cupboard.'

I said, 'But that's got my things in it.'

She said nothing.

'But where will my stuff go?' I said. 'There's nowhere else for me to put it.'

Angela said, 'Well, I don't know, my darling. I haven't really thought about it. Maybe we could fix up a clothes rail or something. We'll find the space somehow.'

But there was no space to be found, and we both knew it. There was nothing for it but to move my things out. 'It's only for the time being, my love,' Angela said, hugging me as I packed up. 'I'm not going to have these things here for ever.'

I didn't make a scene. I packed my clothes and, in order to create more shelf-space, took away my books and music in the cardboard boxes in which the ring binders had arrived. The binders moved in, I moved out. It bothered me, but I knew that I'd be back before long. There was no way I was going to be displaced by chunks of paper.

They're still here. In fact, there are more binders stored here than ever before.

The telephone rings.

It's her. At long last.

'Hello?'

'John,' Rosie says to me. 'Listen, John – do you know where Steve is?'

A numb moment passes and I sigh, 'Rosie.'

She sounds troubled. 'He left the house this afternoon and, well, he hasn't come back.'

I say, 'Right, I see.' I feel a dull surprise, because it is not like Steve to be away from home for any length of time; but that is all I feel.

'I just don't know where he could be,' Rosie says. I can hear her expelling a cloud of smoking breath and then immediately taking another deep drag. 'I've tried ringing his friends, but none of them knows where he is.' Rosie says, 'I don't know what to do, John. This isn't like him. Something's happened to him,' she says.

There is a silence, and I know that Rosie is expecting some comforting words from me. 'Well,' I say, 'how about, how about trying . . .' Then I stop. I do not have a clue where Steve might be and when it comes down to it, well, when it comes down to it I do not care. 'Look,' I say finally, 'don't worry, Rosie, he'll be back. He'll show up sooner or later.'

She is weeping now, but she still manages to say, 'You're heartless, John. I've always said that about you. You just don't give a damn about anybody.'

'Rosie,' I say, 'Rosie, listen, Steve will be – '

But then she hangs up.

Heartless? What does she expect me to do, go out into the rain and find her boyfriend for her? Set up a search party? Spend an hour on the phone commiserating? Bang my head against the wall just because I'm her brother?

I light a cigarette. Maybe I am heartless; but what choice have I got?

Look at what happened on Friday, for God's sake. She came home at about midday and bolted straight past me and Steve to her room, slamming the door behind her and falling on her bed with a dead thud. Two things were shocking. First of all, she seemed to be liquefying: teardrops were travelling over her cheeks down to her chin, her lips shone with run from her nose, and even her fingers were dripping. Then I registered the second thing about her: her hair.

Ah, Rosie's hair . . . Rosie's hair is a family legend. It is packed securely in that suitcase of Breeze myths that is clicked open from time to time at family gatherings, its hand-me-down contents familiar and sentimental and orienting. Rosie's hair is in there with the story of Grandma Breeze's radical feminism as a young woman and the time when she granted asylum in her bedroom cupboard to a suffragette wanted for vandalism; of the number of languages (six: English, Irish, French, German, Italian and Spanish) which my mother's mother, Georgina O'Malley, spoke fluently; of the invention by great-grandfather Breeze of an egg incubator, and of how he failed to patent the invention and missed out on millions.

Rosie's long Irish locks, which when gathered and braided dropped from her head in a thick, fiery rope, have made her stand out like a beacon at baptisms, Christmases and weddings, and be recognized and kissed and admired by distant Breezes who have never met her but who have received word of her flaming head. If I should have children, no doubt they too will learn of the two-foot mane that Aunt Rosie once sported and how one day, the day before yesterday to be precise, Friday, she came home with it cropped down to her skull, dashing past me like a carrot-topped soldier late for parade.

Rosie barricaded herself into her room for the rest of the day. When Steve occasionally emerged from it to fetch her something from the kitchen and left the door ajar, I could hear muffled sobbing. I did not say anything; what was there to say? Pa, though, could not restrain himself when he came round yesterday morning on his way to visiting Merv Rasmussen in hospital.

'Rosie . . . Your hair.'

She said nothing. She was in the kitchen with her back turned to him, busying herself with dishes in the sink. Pa was stock-still, his head tilted sideways, rooted in the hallway like a nail badly hammered into wood.

After a moment he looked up at me. Then he looked at Rosie again and then he looked at me again. He rubbed his face with one hand. He was lost for words, that was obvious. He wanted to say something, but as usual could not think what. No matter what he says or does not say, no matter how gently he treads, his words always seem to snag on Rosie's tripwire sensibilities and blow up in his face. To her chagrin, Rosie, who is always buying him presents and sending him cheerful and amusing postcards from around the world, simply cannot talk to him face-to-face without something going off within her. When that detonation happens, she instinctively produces a wounding remark, retaliating for some nameless injury which my innocent father has caused her to suffer.

So Pa decided not to pursue the matter. He said, with a forced casualness, 'So, who's coming with me to see Merv?'

Not me, I thought. Although I knew Merv, I hardly knew him well enough to visit him in intensive care.

'Well?' Pa said, jingling his keys. He still had not moved from his original spot in the hallway. 'Johnny? Rosie? Are you coming, my love?'

Rosie said from the kitchen, 'Johnny and I don't know him. He's your friend. You see him.'

Pa said, 'But Rosie, my love, the man's at death's door. He needs all the support he can get. He's met you and Johnny. He knows you. He knows you're my children. I'm sure he'd like you to be there.'

Racking up soapy plates with a clatter, Rosie said, 'Don't be ridiculous.' She scrubbed furiously at a frying-pan, rasping it with all of her strength. 'I mean, let's be honest, it won't make any real difference to Johnny or me whether what's his name – Marv? – lives or dies. We hardly know him.' She banged a dish. 'If there's one thing I can't stand it's that kind of hypocrisy.'

Pa flinched. He gripped his car keys and there was a moment of silence.

Then he said, 'Is that what you think, Rosie? Is that really what you think?' He slowly shook his head. 'Well, I'm getting out of here,' he said, disgust in his voice. 'All of you, you all . . .' He did not finish his sentence. He walked out of the front door and made for his car.

'Brilliant, Rosie,' I said. 'Bloody brilliant.'

Rosie turned towards me and shouted, 'Go with him! Don't let him go there alone! Can't you see that he needs someone to go with him? Go on,' she shouted, 'get after him!'

She was right; and I snatched a jacket and ran out into the street and caught up with my father just as he was steering the car out of its parking slot. I opened the front passenger door and got in.

We drove along in silence.

The hospital was situated a few miles to the north, at the top of the hill overlooking the old harbour. It was a dark, cloudy afternoon. The leafing trees shook around in the wind and Rockport and its components – the oily canals, the bunched cranes and, north of the river, the housing towers with balconies flagged with drying clothes – jerked slowly by as we stopped and started.

Two miles and ten log-jammed minutes later, Pa still had not spoken. Usually, when Pa has been hurt by Rosie, he pours his heart out to me. 'What's the matter with that girl?' he asks helplessly. 'She's got everything: she's smart, she's got a good job, and, to cap it all, she's beautiful!' He shakes his head. 'She doesn't mean the things she says, Johnny, not deep down. I know that. It breaks my heart to see her so unhappy. I just don't know what to do about it. I'm at a loss. There's something gnawing away at her and God help me I don't know what it is.' And off he goes, beating a path around the room. 'Is it money? How's she doing for money? Maybe she needs some funds. Here,' he says, taking out a pen and cheque book, 'I want you to give this to her.'

'Pa, don't do that,' I say. I physically stop him from writing the cheque. 'She's fine for money. You know it's not money.'

'What is it, then? Johnny, all I know is that when she was a kid she was a little bundle of dynamite. You'd have to see it to believe it. Do you know that she used to bring your mother and me breakfast in bed? She was just four and half years old.' I know what Pa is going to say next. He is going to say, She used to bring us boiled eggs with our faces drawn on them, can you imagine? 'She used to bring us boiled eggs with our faces drawn on them,' Pa says. 'Can you imagine? Then you used to come in as well, and the two of you kids would jump into bed with us.' Those were glory days for my father, the days when his double bed bulged with all four Breezes. 'I don't know,' Pa says. 'Maybe she misses your mother. A girl needs to have her mother. She really loved Ma, you know, Johnny. The two of them were like two peas in a pod.' Then he says, 'But your mother's not with us, God rest her soul, and what can I do about that?'

But this time Pa was not coming out with all of this. This time he was keeping quiet.

I felt bad. I should have agreed to go with him to the hospital without hesitation.

'What's that noise?' Pa suddenly demanded.

I could hear nothing.

'You hear that? I'm stopping the car.'

'I can't hear a thing,' I said.

'You can't hear that? You can't hear that humming noise?'

'Pa, that's the engine. That's the sound of the engine.'

He pulled over to the side of the road. 'I'm going to have a look,' he said. 'I'm going to open her up.' He stepped out into the wind and raised the bonnet.

I stayed where I was. As usual, Pa was hearing things. Although he drives a Volvo of perfect reliability, my father never stops detecting problems with it and constantly takes it to the garage for unnecessary services and check-ups and all-clears. The cause, I suspect, is this: Pa cannot believe that, unlike almost everything else in his life, his car will not let him down. Far from comforting him, this makes him anxious. Oppressed by the knowledge that this state of affairs cannot last for ever, that trouble simply has to be brewing somewhere in that machine, Pa drives around in a state of fretfulness, waiting for the worst. I just wish that the damn thing would break down and put him out of his misery once and for all.

'Try her now,' Pa shouted from behind the hood.

I switched on the motor. It made a faultless, purring sound.

'OK!' Pa shouted. He leaned over into the engine and made an adjustment. 'OK, try her now!'

Again I turned the key and again the motor sounded like a stroked cat.

Pa slammed down the bonnet and came in out of the wind. 'That should hold her together until I can reach a garage,' he said, putting on his seat belt. 'It was a good thing we stopped. I reckon there's an oil leak in there. It could have seized up at any minute.'

We drove off again. Thanks to the pit stop, the incident

with Rosie no longer fouled the atmosphere, and when a short while later we got held up in more traffic by the docks, I felt able to turn on the car radio. I moved the dial to Station 5, the sports station. John Hall was on, previewing the next day's soccer fixtures. Pa turned up the volume.

'It's the last day of the season,' John Hall said, 'and, the championship having already been won by Clonville, attention will be focused on the relegation clash at the bottom of the First Division between Rockport United and Ballybrew. It's make or break time. Both teams have the same number of points, but United have marginally the better goal difference. They can therefore settle for the draw, whereas Ballybrew need maximum points – a problem, since Ballybrew have yet to win a game away from home this season. My prediction? United to avoid the drop.'

'Let's hope he's right,' Pa said as the car inched forward. The wind had dropped but the sky had darkened further. The wipers were slowly mowing rain from the windshield. Pa tapped the wheel. 'Johnny, what are we doing down there, scratching about with the likes of Ballybrew? A big club like United should be right up there with the Clonvilles, contesting the championship.' We moved forward by a car-length. The rain relentlessly arrived on the windscreen, each surge of droplets wiped out then instantaneously replaced by fresh, momentary troops, in turn effaced in their thousands as the wiper swung back over the glass. 'I remember when United were a great team, when we won the league, the Cup and the Continental Cup in three straight years. I tell you, Johnny, those were the days. What a line-up: Neville Clarke, the Tiger of Antigua, in goal, Guthrie, Knox, Walker and Janusz at the back, Dingemans, Dean and Lazarus in midfield, Loasby, Le Quesne and Newman up front. Sixty thousand for every home match and never once a fight.' Yet again, Pa shook his head. 'You should have seen Redrock Park in those days, Johnny. The stands would be bursting over and the schoolboys would be passed down over our heads to the front of the terraces. The atmosphere was different. You didn't see moats or fences or firecrackers, you didn't see pitch invasions. And the singing . . .' Pa swallowed. 'By God, Johnny, you should have been there to hear the singing.'

I did not reply to this, because I knew that Pa had not been there to hear the singing either. The first time Pa had even taken notice of Rockport United was when I began supporting them as an eight-year-old and when every match day saw his white-fisted, oblivious boy hunched over the radio and transported in its tiny racket to the heart of the ringing stadium, my day, sometimes even my week, hinged precariously on the game's outcome. Out of sympathy, Pa became a Rockport United fan, too. He enrolled me in the supporters' club and then, to keep me company, put his own name down. He bought me all of the gear so that I could listen to the game properly kitted out: the strip, the red and white scarf, the bobble hat incorporating the club's famous symbol, the prancing red lambs. Pa bought a club rattle and he bought a pair of lucky underpants to wear on Cup days. Why he thought those underpants – red and white checks – were lucky, I do not know, because in all of the time that he wore them United never won a thing. But that did not deter him. Every season the Cup would start afresh, every year Pa pulled on those shorts and every year United got knocked out.

Christmas Day, 1979. I am twelve years old, Pa is forty-two and there is my mother in her blue apron, temporarily leaving the last turkey that she will ever cook to watch her children open their presents. There, under the Christmas tree, is a record with my name, *Johnny,* written on the wrapper between the sledges and the snowmen. Eagerly I rip open the package, hoping for the album that all my classmates are listening to – *Spare Head: I Shouldn't Have Eaten That Second Banana* – but it is not to be. What I have instead is a recording of the 1968 Continental Cup final, when on a hot and floodlit Parisian night United beat Lisbon 4–1 after extra time to win the trophy.

Pa swoops as I kneel there, removing my gift from my hand. 'This is brilliant,' he says, clumsily dropping the disc on the turntable. 'This,' Pa says, 'is what I call *brilliant*.'

He listens to the record – both sides – maybe three times that day, and that day the house resonates with the euphoria of one hundred thousand supporters of Rockport United. Each time a goal is scored my father's arms half rise in joy and a great smile cracks across his face; then, quickly, before the cheering has died down, he darts over to the record-player, returns the needle by a fraction of an inch, switches up the volume by a notch or two and listens to it one more time.

My father is scoring goals at will. *It's there!* the commentator cries again and again. *It's there! It's there!*

6

The windowpanes clank and shudder in the wind. I take a look outside. It's still raining, and still there's no sign of Angie; no sign of anyone in the street except a young boy on a bicycle, standing up on the pedals and swaying from side to side as he climbs into the gale. The windows shudder again, clattering violently this time, as though rocked by a tremor.

Well, at least that's one thing I can rest assured about: quakes. No movement of the earth's crust has ever been recorded in Rockport and that, according to Steve, is a fact. I'm happy to believe him. Thanks to his new-found enthusiasm for the *Time-Life* pamphlets about natural disasters, Steve actually knows something about planetary spasms. It's not the first time he has mastered a peculiar field of expertise. He used to be an authority on new consumer goods, the novelty products advertised in the morning junk mail that puddled in the hallway door every morning. Steve used to peruse those catalogues for hours, lost in a world of doggy boot-scrapers, portable intercom door-chimes, sonic mole-chasers, therapeutic putty and extra-loud personal alarms, dreaming, perhaps, of – well, who knows what he was dreaming of? Now, though, the innovation reports have been supplanted in his imagination by the *Time-Life* pamphlets offering books about the inimical forces of nature. Although Steve has never bought a page of the menacing literature on offer, he enjoys reading about reading it. There is one particular leaflet, called 'Storm (Discover the Deadly Forces That Shape Our World)', which he consults time after time.

'God, just listen to this,' he said one time. 'This is just amazing. Just listen to this.' He started to recite the text in a painstaking monotone. ' "Man lives at the bottom of a dense and turbulent sea of gases. Ten miles deep, the atmosphere is constantly in motion; and when one mass collides with another, the skies erupt, scouring the earth and purging the atmosphere with unbridled fury. The result," ' Steve quoted, ' "is storm . . ." '

At this point I left the room to make myself a coffee, but there was to be no escape. Steve raised his voice for my benefit, so that even from the kitchen I continued to hear his intonings.

' "In 1938 a hurricane veered away from its expected path and cut into the East Coast of America. At a windspeed of 120 mph it cut a swathe between New York and Boston leaving over 600 dead, 60,000 homeless and caused damage estimated (1938 values) at over a third of a billion dollars." ' Steve paused to assimilate these statistics. ' "On December 8 1963, a bolt of lightning struck a 707 jet sending it plummeting to the ground in a ball of flame. Eighty-two people died." God,' Steve said. ' "These natural catastrophes are evidence of the deadly power of man's oldest enemy, and demonstrates that with all our advanced technology, our satellites and computers, we are always at the mercy of mighty, ever-threatening forces." ' Steve put down the leaflet. 'God,' he said again in a dazed voice.

It is possible that this apocalyptic material provides a clue to why Steve is so indisposed to leave the flat. Perhaps he regards Rockport – a wholesome, unperilous city in the general view – as an environment of native wantonness. Maybe this is why he adheres so devoutly to the inside world: because he has seen through Rockport, that comfortable haven, seen through its façade of well-being, its superficies of bottlebanks and grass-anchored dunes, of cycling lanes, malls, shipyards and open-air skating-rinks, of pike-stocked canals and theatres, of all-ticket football matches, academic symposia, stinking fish-markets, parks sprinkled with deck-chairs and bars pouring out pint after black pint of thick stout. Maybe Steve has identified all of these as mere phenomena and maybe, in accordance with some privately held epistemology, he has discovered that things are not as ordered and purposeful as they might seem; that Rockport, like the boiling Venus of his pamphlets, is in essence a place of hostility. Maybe, in the light of this alarming data, he is simply holing up, keeping his head below the parapet, in the hope that Rockport, like some passing storm, will somehow blow over.

Maybe; but I doubt it. I think that you have got closer to the bottom of the matter once you have recognized that Stephen Manus is a member of that old-fashioned psychological species: the lazybones.

But who I am to criticize him for doing nothing?

A month or so ago I was in the basement, smoking a cigarette, and although as usual the door was closed, through the floorboards I could hear the voices directly above me, in the sitting-room.

Pa's voice: 'What's the matter with him? Why won't he let anyone go down there? Every time I come around he's locked away like a hermit.'

Rosie's voice: 'Pa, take a plate, would you? You're spilling crumbs everywhere.'

'Sorry, my love.' Then, after a pause, 'Is he always like this? Look at the time. It's seven-thirty. If he carries on like this he'll burn himself out.'

Rosie says, 'Don't talk nonsense. You know as well as I do that he's not doing a thing down there.'

Pa says, 'I wish you wouldn't say these things, Rosie, my love. You're being harsh.'

'Well, how many chairs have you seen recently?' There's a long pause.

'I'm telling you, Rosie, you're wrong,' Pa says. 'John's a grafter, he always has been. Remember how he got stuck into his accountancy exams? Remember how hard he worked to set up his exhibition?'

'I don't want to argue about this. You believe what you want to.'

'But, Rosie, if you're right, then we've got a problem; and if we've got a problem, we've got to do something about it.'

Rosie laughs drily. '*We* haven't got a problem, Pa. *He* has.' Raising her voice, she says, 'Pa, *don't* look at me like that. What am I supposed to do? Make the chairs for him? Am I supposed to get the glue and get the wood and get whatever *shit* he keeps down there and do it myself?'

'Keep your voice down, he'll hear you.'

'What do I care? It's about time we had some truth around here. I'm sick of it, sick of all this pretence.' Now she's shouting. 'He's crap, Pa. Your son is crap. He's a *crappy furniture-maker.*'

'Rosie. Stop it.'

But she keeps on shouting. 'He's a waste of money. He's a waste of space and you know it.'

Pa shouts down the stairs, 'Don't listen to her, John, it's not true, she's just being spiteful!'

'Prove me wrong, Johnny,' Rosie shouts. 'Bring up a chair and prove me wrong.'

'Don't do it, John!' Pa shouts. 'You don't have to prove anything! Do you hear me? You don't have to prove a thing, son!'

I stay where I am, behind the locked door.

I can't prove Rosie wrong. I haven't made a chair in six months.

But it isn't laziness. If only it were.

I'm ashamed about it. I daren't mention it to anyone – not even to Angela; at least, not now.

Things have changed since Angela and I started off four years ago. I am no longer the budding professional she met and she is no longer the provincial student on a holiday job whom I managed to impress. In the course of the intervening years, Angela Flanagan has become a high-flier. She has accumulated more degrees and diplomas than all of the Breezes put together – a BSc in economics, an MSc in statistics and an MBA. The result is that six months ago she landed her job at Bear Elias, the management consultants. As I understand it, she's part of a team of brainstormers that visits disorganized organizations – often furtively – in order to recommend their reorganization. Angela loves her work and does it very well, and not long ago she was promoted to number two in the team. Professionally, things are coming along just fine for her.

Pa holds her in awe. He seeks out her opinion on various matters with great seriousness. 'What are the prospects, Angela, of an early recovery from the recession?' Or, 'Is it true that the poverty of the Third World is the most vital economic challenge of all?' 'She's something else, that Angela,' he says to me in a hushed voice when she has temporarily left the room. 'So intelligent, so well educated. A fine young woman,' he says. 'Just the sort of person we're crying out for at the Network. A few more like her and we'd turn the whole thing around.' Angela returns, and Pa again assumes a shy, almost humble posture. She, of course, is embarrassed, and does her best to put him at his ease by giving him modest and respectful answers. She likes Pa a lot. 'He's wonderful, your father,' she said to me after they first met. And then she put her arms around me and kissed me fully on the mouth. 'Just like his son,' she whispered.

As a result of Angela's success at Bear Elias, Pa, like me, has had less opportunity to enjoy her company. I don't resent this one bit – I am delighted, I really am, that Angela is prospering to such a degree; nothing brings me more joy than the proud pleasure she derives from her work – but there is, inevitably, a flip side. While Angela has been on the up and up, I have been on the slide. The disparity is not trivial. Winners do not stick around for ever with losers. I also suspect that there comes a time when a woman takes a cold look at her partner and asks herself whether this is the man she wants to father her children. I walk over to the mirror. I do not see, in the rather shambling figure with the Breeze sloping shoulders reflected there, a likely paterfamilias.

But then I don't hold myself out as promising fatherly material. Although, at the beginning, we toyed like every new couple with the notion of a baby and tried out names for fantastical offspring, I've since made my position clear: I'm not bringing another soul into this world, not if I can help it. As far as I'm concerned, the Breezes have reached the end of the line. I said so in terms only three months ago: this is where the Breezes get off.

'But why?' Angela said. 'Why, my darling?'

We were seated at that table there and had just finished eating. I pushed at my empty plate and picked up my glass of red wine. 'It's not justifiable,' I said. 'When you look at what's going on, when you consider how, how, you know, how . . .' My voice broke. I speechlessly waved my hand and drank a mouthful of wine. 'I don't know, Angie, bringing some poor defenceless kid into the world just so that we could have something to do with our lives . . .' I looked into the blues of her eyes. 'I just don't think I'm cut out for it,' I said. 'So many things can go wrong. I mean, look at Pa. Look at what he goes through. I just couldn't take it.'

'Johnny, he's happy. You could do a lot worse than have what your father has.'

'That's what worries me.'

She filled my glass. 'But without a family, what have you got?' There was affectionate tolerance in her face as she humoured me.

I said, 'You've got a clear conscience, because you haven't inflicted life on anybody.'

She saw I was serious and came over and sat on my lap, her left arm hooked around my neck, her lips brushing lightly against my brow. 'Really, Johnny? Is that how you really feel?'

I nodded. I was holding her tightly by the waist, my hand against her skin beneath her blouse. Her skin is always so warm.

'But things aren't really that bad, are they? Hmm?' She kissed the corner of my mouth. 'Don't look so glum. Come on, cheer up, you're making me feel sad.' I stayed seated, holding her, drawing strength from her heat.

She said, 'Johnny, it's not good. It's not good.'

Like a deer emerging from forest into a space of light, a truth enters a mental clearing: there is no way that Angela will ever become a Breeze.

I crush out my cigarette and go to the kitchen and pour myself a glass of water. Then I remain standing there like a man recovering from a run, both hands pushing against the edge of the work surface, head down, shoulders hunched.

I go to the lavatory. I wash my hands. I find myself back in the empty living-room.

When I telephoned her at work on Friday, I didn't press her for a timetable of her movements this weekend. I wasn't going to ask her to account for her activities – why should I? Angela would go her way and I would go mine, and we would meet up at her flat at nine o'clock.

So why isn't she here?

She could, I suppose, be working. This past fortnight has seen her going flat-out on one of her projects – don't ask me which one – and in fact I haven't laid eyes on her for a week.

Every time I have rung her at the office to fix something up, an obstacle has arisen.

'I don't think so, darling, not tonight. I'm working late.'

'OK,' I say. 'How about tomorrow night?'

'Darling, I'm working tomorrow night, too. I'm not sure when I'll be back. And I just wouldn't be any fun, I'd just come home and flop out.'

I swallow my disappointment. I cannot bring myself to say anything. These are not easy times and I need her. I need every hand on deck.

Angela detects my upset. 'How's work going?' she says.

'OK,' I say shortly. 'Same as ever.' There is a silence as I compose myself. Then I say, 'Well, then, how about . . .'

She interrupts me. 'I've got to go now,' she says in the flat voice she uses when someone comes into her office. 'Speak to you later, OK?'

That is how it has been all week.

She could be seeing someone else. At this very moment she could be seeing another man.

No. There is no way that she would ever two-time me. Not Angela. If there's one person in the world I can bank on not to let me down, it's her. I *know* her: she's not the type to cheat. She's open and straightforward. Any time that there has been a problem, she has come straight out with it.

But maybe she has changed. Maybe she has hardened, like her body. This year, thanks to her work-outs at the fitness club, Angela's physique, like land visited by a glacier, has been smoothened, transformed from soft bumpy terrain into an unfamiliar plain of muscle. Normally, of course, this would be cause for erotic celebration and renewal; but there's something aloof about that revamped body – the taut, independent stomach, the unmalleable buttocks, the tense, untrembling thighs – which makes me nervous. That body is under new management, and I'm not the reason why.

7

It doesn't bear thinking about.

But then, right now, what does? This afternoon – does that bear thinking about?

Too shaken up by the incident with the midget to drive the car, Pa let me chauffeur him home. 'Just take it easy on the gear changes,' he said as I removed the keys from the pocket of his anorak. He eased himself into his seat with difficulty and tiredly strapped his belt across his chest. 'Go slowly,' he said, then fell back and closed his eyes. By the time I had accelerated into the main road and found a niche in the traffic, he was fast asleep. He sat in a sideways slump, his head knocking slightly against the shivering window, his breath expelled in a slow, regular gasp. I felt a warm gladness that he was slumbering there, in the comfort of his car, that he had found a secure respite from the day's brutalities. He looked so vincible, with his cornered shrunken body and his powerless hands. When we get home I'll run him a hot bath and make him some soup, I decided. Yes, and maybe I'll fix him one of those salami and gherkin sandwiches that he likes. Then, with beers at hand and the Sunday newspapers scattered about and Trusty nuzzling at our feet, we'll settle back and watch the United game on TV. That should see him right, I thought.

About five minutes later, Pa woke up.

'Can you hear that, Johnny?'

I said, 'Pa, take it from me, there's nothing wrong with the car, all right? Now go back to sleep.'

'No,' he said, 'not the car. Listen to that.'

Then I heard it, too: the sound of the crowd at Redrock Park, its cries and handclaps amplified by the acoustical stadium and carried by the wind over rooftops to Pa and me, sitting in a car almost a mile away. I lowered the window a touch. *We love United*, they were singing, *We love United, we do, oh, United, we love you.* And then, euphorically, *Here we go, here we go, here we go . . .*

'Just listen to that,' Pa said. 'What an atmosphere. And there's still half an hour to go before the kick-off. Look at those crowds,' he said, pointing to groups of fans walking quickly across the road. Studying his watch, he said, 'We'll be home in five or ten minutes. For a quick wash and a bite before it starts.' For a moment we continued to look at his timepiece with the built-in referee's stopwatch, figuring out his schedule, and then with a vigorous rubbing of hands he exclaimed, 'Johnny, I can feel it in my bones, we're going to win today, we're going to win!' He looked at me with a grin, and when I caught his eye we both burst out laughing. 'That's right!' Pa said, joyously assuming a hillbilly American accent, 'we're going to whup their asses, boy!'

I drove on through the familiar bends of the road home, amazed at how swiftly my father had recovered from the morning's degradations. Just twenty minutes ago he had been spat in the face and insulted, and less than an hour before that he had been sexually assaulted by a terrier and publicly reviled. Yet here he was again, restored to enthusiasm. Was there no limit to his resilience?

It could only be that this ability to recuperate and rally was a product of Pa's faithfulness. Pa is the most faithful person I know. There is no thing or person which he does not believe in. God and the life hereafter, the future well-being of his children, the success of his football team, the loyalty of his dog, the reliability of Whelan, the potential of Steve, the value of employment, the upturn in the housing market: come what may, Pa has been absolutely trusting and hopeful in respect of all of these glassy entities. No matter how often and violently they shatter on the floor and how irreparable their fragmentation, by a mystery of fidelity the smithereens are always reconstituted in Pa's mind. But where does this credulous optimism come from? Is it a necessary biological witlessness, a natural reality-blocker secreted by some gland in the brain? Or does it arrive from some occult, immaterial source?

I enjoyed my father's crazy hopefulness while it lasted, because it would, of course, be followed by a crazy nervous fearfulness that his hopes would be dashed, and I knew that before long the confidence would drain from him and he would be transformed into a wreck barely able to remain in the same room as the televised football match, that he would stand rooted at the doorway to the kitchen, a man appalled and mesmerized by a scene of horror, half watching the action through the fingers clasping his white face as the opposition advanced on the United goal like zombies from a nightmare . . .

I pulled up in front of the house. Although we were in a hurry, Pa remained seated for a moment and breathed, as he often does when he arrives at his front door, Home sweet home. I think that he can be forgiven this sentimentalism. That building – a detached three-storeyed suburban house with a garden, green-railed balconies at the front and back, a pear tree, two lilac trees, double garage, clambering roses and four bedrooms – has been the asylum of the Breezes for almost twenty years.

We walked up the path to the front door, which I unlocked and pushed open. Then we saw it: a pile of shit on the floor at the bottom of the staircase. We looked at each other: Trusty.

I said heavily, 'Don't worry about it. I'll fix it. You go on upstairs and have your bath.'

Before I went to fetch the tissues, scrubber and carpet shampoo, I went to the sitting-room to switch on the television. I did not want to risk missing a minute of the game. I picked up the remote control, aimed it at the corner of the room, and punched the button.

Nothing happened. The television was not there. I realized instantly, even before I noticed that the curtains were billowing in the broken-open french windows, that there had been a burglary. I wiped my face with my hand. Then I called upstairs. 'Pa, can you come down?'

'What?' he asked nervously as he descended the stairs in his socks and track suit. 'What's the matter?'

I said nothing. I just led him into the living-room.

'What's happened?' Pa said. 'Where's the TV? Where's the CD?' He turned around on the spot. 'But that's impossible,' he said. 'There's a safety catch on those windows. Whelan put it there himself. And there's an alarm – why isn't the alarm ringing?'

He walked over to the french windows and tried to drag them shut, but the hinges had been broken. The draught kept pouring through and the living-room fluttered like a field. 'I just don't understand this,' Pa said. 'What about Trusty? How could she let this happen? Where is she, anyway?'

There was a silence as we stood there trying to take things in.

'Well,' I said, 'I guess we can forget about watching the game.'

Pa was not listening. He was moving his palm over the vacant mantelpiece in a slow caress. He raised his hand to his face and blankly regarded his powdery fingertips. The photographs. The one-and-only, silver-framed family photographs had been removed. The famous honeymoon picture; the last remaining picture of my father's mother, a young woman in the 1920s leaning confidently against a car upon which the photographer, his head under the hood of his camera, has cast his shadow; long-haired Rosie at her first communion; me, a ten-year-old in my Rovers kit, drinking juice during the half-time break with my team-mates; and several others that I can't bring back. Holiday snapshots, most of them, nothing special when they were up there. The usual lucky moments captured in the usual way.

Pa sat down wordlessly. Upstairs, the falling bathwater thundered against enamel.

I went up and turned off the taps. When I returned downstairs, he was still sitting, looking dumbly ahead of him. 'Pa,' I said. I touched him on the shoulder. 'Your bath's ready.'

He got to his feet. He slowly walked up the stairs. He went into his bedroom and closed the door behind him.

I got on to the telephone and rang the police.

'I suppose we'd better send somebody over,' the switchboard operator said. 'We'll have someone there within half an hour.'

'Should I touch anything?' I said.

The officer sighed. 'Look, if you want us to carry out a

forensic examination and the rest of it, then I suppose you should leave things as they are. But frankly, Mr Breeze . . .'

'I understand,' I said.

'I mean, there are so many break-ins these days,' he said apologetically. 'Besides, you don't really want us camped in your house for hours, do you?'

'Don't worry,' I said. 'Thanks,' I said.

The first thing to do was clear up Trusty's mess. But where was Trusty? Outside, most probably, looking for some action. Trusty was on heat, and although she is only two years old, when she is on heat, she's hot. If you even half open a window or a door she will be through it like a shot, frenzied by her lust. There are many evenings which Pa and I have spent combing the neighbourhood gardens where that dog engages in her trysts, whistling and calling her name in the moonlight: Trusty! Trusty! And when we do finally spy her, she snarls furiously and makes another dash for it through the hedges. The scenario of Trusty's disappearance was therefore obvious: instead of recognizing the intruder for the enemy he was, she had welcomed him as a rescuer and had bolted through the french windows he had cracked open. So much for the BEWARE OF THE DOG sign which Pa had posted at the front and back of the house.

I have my theory as to why Trusty has turned out this way. At the time of her very first period in heat, Pa and I took her for a walk in the field near the house. Trusty was still young and innocent and had barely learned to walk without treading on her long ears. So there she was, hopping over the grassy earth with her nose to the ground, eagerly inhaling the novel smells, when a large muscular animal, an Alsatian, ran up to her and fucked her without hesitation. Then it ran off.

We had all been helpless – Pa, Trusty and I. Pa had a go at pulling off the Alsatian by the collar, I shouted and waved and threw sticks, Trusty wriggled and fought. But the police dog stuck to its guns and we were forced to watch as Trusty, a dazed look in her beseeching, unconsenting brown eyes, was raped by a beast twice her size. I think that this shocking experience, which should have turned Trusty off sex altogether, probably had the opposite effect. I think that it turned her into the libidinist that she is.

Once I had tidied the living-room there was nothing for it but to clean up in the hallway. I retrieved the necessary equipment from the broom cupboard and approached the pile of excrement, which for some reason looked odd. I scraped it up quickly, leaving only a faint stain on the floor. Just as I was getting out the carpet shampoo, the door rang: the cops.

I opened the door to two uniformed constables, a man and a woman. The woman was the senior of the two. She looked around and asked the questions while her colleague wrote down my replies in his notebook. 'This stuff that's been stolen,' she said, 'is it yours? Or is it your dad's?' She wandered over to the french windows.

'My father's,' I said.

'Is he in?'

'He's upstairs,' I said. 'Up in his bedroom.' (This wasn't like him – he normally would have been the first to greet the forces of law and order.)

'Could we have a word with him?' the policewoman asked, peering out into the garden. 'We have to take a statement.'

I'll get him, I said, and ran up.

But Pa was not in his bedroom. I went out on to the landing and said, 'Pa?' and there was no reply; but then, as I quietened, I heard a snuffling noise from the third floor. I went up the stairs. 'Pa?'

I stood still. There it was again: snuff, sniff, snuff. I pushed open the door to Rosie's old bedroom – the bedroom with the big skylight and the blue-flowered wallpaper and the piles of children's books.

It was him all right. He was standing in the no man's land between the bed and the wall, his head turned away towards the corner of the room. He was still in his track suit. On the bed was an old, torn bin-liner and a scattering of photographs. As Pa drew his sleeve across his nose he sniffed again, and the daylight caught his face and I saw that his eyes were more red and glistening and swollen than ever.

I went across to the bed, to the photographs. These were the leftovers – the last pictorial records of the Breezes in our possession. They were also the worst ones. The clear, lovely pictures – of my mother holding the hands of her two children one snowy winter, of summer picnics, of my parents at the altar – had been taken by Rosie just before she went to university and collected in a marvellous album. Then Rosie, in the way that she mislays all of the gold rings and heirlooms that she is given, lost the album. No one blamed her, but for months afterwards she would burst into tears of bereavement at the thought of those essential images being gone for ever. Now that Pa's silver-framed photos had gone, those snapshots on Rosie's old bed were, apart from our memories, the remaining threads to the family's past. I took a look at them. There was only one picture left of my mother: seated on a patio somewhere – at a friend's house, I supposed; I did not recognize the background – my mother's face is plunged into darkness, the photographer (Pa, no doubt) having made the mistake of shooting into sunlight. All you can make out of her is the curled outline of a 1960s haircut and the silhouetted knees, crossed; apart from a chin and nose which show as flecks in the gloom, she is faceless.

I checked the bin-liner once more, but no, that was all that remained of Ma. There were no other pictures of her.

I put the photos back into the bin-liner and touched his shoulder. 'Pa,' I said. 'Pa, the police are downstairs,' I said.

He followed me down.

The policewoman asked him the same questions she had asked me. He replied in a toneless voice, after lengthy pauses, looking stupidly into space. Meanwhile, the other policeman had started sniffing around – literally. His nostrils were twitching, as if he had caught the whiff of something.

'Thank you very much, Mr Breeze,' the policewoman said gently. 'Your father's still in a state of shock,' she said to me.

The policeman whispered something in her ear. In response, she too began breathing in sharply.

'It's the dog,' I said with embarrassment. I pointed to the stain in the hallway. 'We have a dog. I haven't had time to clean all of it up yet.'

They looked at each other, then examined the traces ingrained in the carpet. Then they looked at each other again.

'You sure, sir?' the policewoman asked. 'You sure it's the dog?'

'Well, yes. I mean, what else . . .'

'You see, sir,' the policewoman said, looking me in the eye for the first time, 'it's, well, it's becoming something of a thing for burglars to, well, defecate in the house they've robbed. It's like their signature.'

Their signature?

The policeman, meanwhile, kneeled down and snipped a few of the darkened threads and placed them in a little plastic bag. 'Exhibit A,' he said.

I washed the carpet as soon as they left. Then I ran Pa a fresh bath and made sure he undressed and got into it. I went to the kitchen and made us some sandwiches and tea. When, quarter of an hour later, Pa, an in-and-out bather, had not yet come down, I went up to see what was going on.

He was still in the bath, lying hip-deep in the shallow, lukewarm water, his torso completely dry. He did not turn when I came in.

'Are you OK?' I said.

He turned his eyes – one pointed at me, one at the shower-curtain – and blinked: in the affirmative, I thought.

'I've made some tea and sandwiches,' I said.

He stirred, his knees sploshily displacing water, but he did not get up. The movement sent red and green and white trails of dissolved soap smoking up through the bathwater. Pa has this habit of gumming together the slivers of used soap into a multicoloured bar, like an Italian ice-cream.

He raised his elbows and took hold of the rim of the tub, perfect, shiny particles of water starrily clustered on the silver and black hairs of his armpits. Then he let go and slid back down the slope of the tub, the skin of his bottom making a squeak.

'Come on,' I said softly, my hands under his armpits, smelling for the first time in a long time the tang of my father. I hauled up his dripping, aged form – the tender pectorals, the diminished penis, the gleaming, brittle shinbones. It was palpable, the terrible vicinity of death.

I dropped a large towel over his shoulders. 'You go on ahead,' I said.

I pulled the plug and the water began to sluice away, stranding green and red nuggets of soap on the white floor of the bath.

8

If Whelan, of Whelan Lock & Key, 24–hour Service, had done his job properly – if he had repaid the faith which Pa had shown in him – that burglary would probably never have taken place. All it needed was a half-decent lock on those french windows and an alarm that actually worked. But Whelan messed up. It doesn't surprise me. The man is hopeless. For seven days now I have been imploring him on the phone to come round and fit new locks on the front door of the flat, and for seven days – and in spite of three appointments – he has failed to show. The last time I spoke to him was on Friday, immediately after Pa's anxious call. Although Whelan had let me down twice already, I decided to have another crack at it. Third time lucky, I figured. Besides, I wanted an explanation for his conduct.

'Mr Whelan, I waited for you all morning yesterday,' I said.

'Yesterday morning, was it?' Whelan enquired. There was genuine curiosity in his voice.

'We'd made an appointment,' I said.

'Number 47, was it?'

It was. I did not say anything.

'I remember now,' Whelan said. 'It's all coming back to me now. Yes, that's right. I came round in the afternoon, but there was no reply when I rang. Yes, I remember now,' Whelan said.

'Mr Whelan,' I said tiredly, 'I was in all afternoon.'

Whelan said, 'Were you? Well, isn't that a strange thing?'

Desperately, I said, 'How about this afternoon? Can you come this afternoon?'

Whelan sucked in air. 'This afternoon is hard, Mr Breeze. Very hard. It would have to be tomorrow, Saturday. It would have to be Saturday.'

I had to get the door fixed. Saturday, I agreed. Ten o'clock.'

'I'll be there, Mr Breeze,' Whelan guaranteed. 'Count on it.'

Today is Sunday. Still no sign of Whelan.

Yesterday morning, while waiting for that joker, I forced myself to go down into the basement workshop. As usual, it was so gloomy that I had to switch on the light, weakly diffused by a naked bulb hanging from the ceiling. I sat down on a box and lit a cigarette and stared at the lifeless shapes of my works in progress. This lasted about a minute. Then I looked up at the barred, dirt-smudged window: dustbins and, looming behind and blotting out the sky, the hedge, dark with new leaves. I groggily bolted back upstairs.

I went to the kitchen and made myself a double-strength cup of coffee. I flicked another cigarette out of the packet. A thin sweat started filming my upper lip. Just a month previously, this telephone conversation had taken place with the gallery owner.

'How's it going, John?' Simon Devonshire said.

'Great,' I said. 'Just great.'

'So, when do we get to see your stuff? We're all very excited, you know.'

'You'll get it soon,' I said. 'Don't worry, it's all under control.'

Devonshire laughed and said, 'It had better be. I'd like the chairs within the next week or two. We need to photograph them for the catalogue.'

The catalogue? 'The catalogue?'

'We're going to have to have a meeting about that,' Devonshire said, 'to discuss the philosophy that underpins your work. People will want to know what they're looking at.'

'My philosophy.' I swallowed. 'Yes, of course,' I said.

Devonshire laughed again – as far as I could tell, Devonshire was always laughing. He said, 'Don't worry, John, we'll think of something. Leave the theorizing to us. You just concentrate on finishing those pieces and we'll look after the rest.'

Then, two weeks later, we met for lunch. We sat on a grassy slope by a fountain in a small park in the city centre. I had made up my mind to break the news to him with these words: Simon, there's something I have to tell you. I have no chairs. I'm sorry, I've tried, but there it is: it hasn't worked out.

It was a hot spring day, nineteen or twenty degrees, and Devonshire was elated. 'Just look at that,' he said, gesturing grandly at the sun. 'And look at those bastards,' he said, pointing at a brilliant gathering of trees in flower. 'Extraordinary. Absolutely bloody extraordinary.'

I dutifully looked at the magnolias. There was a forceful charm about Devonshire which made him difficult to resist. Although in his mid-forties and, as a gallery owner of real influence, possessed of a certain amount of absolute power, with his enthusiasm, straw-coloured hair and animated expression he still had an uncorrupted, boyish demeanour. His gold-buttoned blazer discarded on the grass and his cotton shirt flapping out of his jeans, he sat down insouciantly in the sunlight and with a groan of comfort unwrapped a smoked salmon sandwich. He took a giant bite and half of the sandwich disappeared. 'So, Johnny, I take it that we can pick up the stools this afternoon.'

'Well, not quite,' I said. I paused. 'Simon, there's something I have to tell you.' I looked at the tips of my shoes.

'What is it?' he said, his mouth still full. 'What's the matter?'

I thought I detected a note of personal concern in his voice. I raised my head to speak and looked him in the face. I had made a mistake. There was nothing solicitous in those eyes. There was only pure threat.

Shocked, I fell momentarily silent; nevertheless, looking again at the ground, I forced out what I had to say.

Devonshire said, 'What do you mean, you won't be ready for another two to three weeks? The show's four weeks away. The catalogue needs to be ready next week.'

I was silent. I made a feckless gesture with my hands.

Crumpling wrapping paper in his fist, Devonshire stood up and sat on the ledge of the fountain. Momentarily he just regarded me, wiping his mouth with a paper tissue. Behind him, a team of rusty fishes spurted loops of glistening water into the air. Then he said, 'One week, Johnny. That's all I'm giving you.' He stood up and turned his back to me and tilted up to the sun. 'Otherwise, my boy, you're going to compensate me for my loss. Do you understand?'

I did not like the sound of that word – *compensate*.

Devonshire turned unhurriedly and picked up his jacket. 'One week,' he said. 'Don't let yourself down, Johnny,' he said.

That week expired last Monday, the day when I left this message with his assistant: Tell Mr Devonshire the chairs will be ready by next Monday. Guaranteed.

Next Monday is tomorrow; which is why, yesterday morning, after I had finished my coffee and cigarette, I forced myself down the stairs into the basement for a second time. There they were, in the gloom, the five unfinished stools I had started making six months ago – *5 Tripods*, they were named. Superficially, they looked fine: five stools, each with wooden seats of a slightly different design, each supported by the same three curved metallic legs. But those legs were the problem. They were unbalanced – so unbalanced that the stools would not stand up. The moment you removed them from the supporting wall, that was it: crash, over they went, in a slow, certain topple. My blunder, of course, was that in my impetuosity I had assembled the chairs without first checking their stability. Stability I had taken for granted.

My task was clear. I had to redesign the legs while nevertheless leaving the chairs' present structure intact, since it was too late to start wholly afresh. Then I had to drive the chairs over to Devonshire's. All this within forty-eight hours. That deadline was my trump card. I was counting on time to spur me to action.

Using a model, I desperately experimented with the addition of a fourth leg – a wooden leg, it had to be, because I had run out of stainless steel. Not only did it look terrible, but the glue I used to secure the leg to the seat simply did not hold. Every time I tried to place a weight upon the seat, off came the leg. Never mind, Johnny, I said to myself after the third failure, try again. Stick at it. Persevere. Never say die. I cleaned the wood, reapplied the glue and pressed the parts together once more. I stayed frozen there for minutes, my face reddening with determination. This time it was going to work. This time . . .

I gently released my grip. After giving the adhesive time to take, I turned the stool up and gingerly stood it on its four legs. So far so good. It stayed up. Then came the moment of truth. I took a thick cabinet-making manual and gently placed it on the seat. I waited. Nothing happened. The chair remained upright. It worked.

I had done it. The stool may have been ugly, but it was a stool; it was better than nothing. All that remained was to affix this fourth leg to the actual chairs, and then I'd be home and dry. Blankly, I lit a cigarette. I couldn't believe it. After so many fruitless months, the nightmare was over. The show would bomb, of course, but at least it would go on. From a legal point of view, if nothing else, I was in the clear.

I heard a creaking noise. I turned around. It was the model chair, and like a foal doing its unsteady splits, it was slowly collapsing as the wooden leg gave way underneath it. With a thick report the book thudded to the ground, followed by the seat, with a crash. Shit, I shouted. Fucking, bloody, fucking *shit*.

I flung my cigarette at the wall and heeled it to a crumbling butt. Sweating with anger, an idea occurred to me. I would cut the legs in half and use the extra metal tubing to provide a triangular lateral base. Yes, that was it! I'd chop the suckers in half! Let's see how they'd like that! But just as I was poised to ignite the blue flame of the blowtorch, I envisaged the end product: crippled, squat, ugly seats that were neither one thing nor the other; stools that fell between two bloody stools. I removed my safety goggles and dropped the cutter. I looked up at the window's dark rectangle and said out loud, That's it. To hell with it. I give up.

Strengthlessly, I sat down on the box again. The day of the exhibition, 16 May, was approaching with every passing second and there was nothing I could do about it. Inevitability had snared me, bagged and unstruggling. I was caught.

And there is another irony – another twist apparent in retrospect: the very reason I started making chairs in the first place was precisely to evade this – the trap of certainty. It was not accountancy I wanted to escape from, it was the guaranteed future it offered. Even from where I stood, half-way through my traineeship, I could see the whole of the way ahead – a road without corners, straight and relentless as a highway through wheatfields, one that took you cleanly through bright and glassy distances, through exams, years in junior and middle management, a partnership in a small firm, through a mortgage and kids and retirement and through, finally and blindingly, to the end. The end! It hit me night after night. No matter how tired or drowsy I was and no matter how many sheep I counted, inevitably it flapped down towards me as I lay there in the distractionless dark; and then it suddenly arrived, all claws – *that* realization. The repercussions were physical. My entire organism was thrown into confoundment: something catapulted in my gut, my face flushed with heat, my brain dispatched furious signals to my extremities. Most strongly of all, though, in the midst of this panic, I felt hoodwinked. Most of all I felt like a man stung by a terrible con.

I would leap out of bed in horror. I would hit all of the lights, grab a cigarette and begin walking around in my bare feet, trying to clear my mind. I would switch on the radio and, if things were really bad, the television, trying to find a late-night movie or game show, anything. Only when Angela lay with me, when, the warm freight of her breasts in my hands, I glued her to me for the long duration of the night, were things any better. But it was not enough – a man cannot lead the life of a limpet. So I turned my hobby into my career. The make-or-break, one-day-at-a-time life of a chair-maker, I reasoned, would be a life of corners, of hairpin twists and turns. There would be no long view. There would be nothing in sight but the job in hand.

Fat chance. I was like the prisoner who lowers himself down on a rope of bedsheets only to discover that he has escaped into the punishment wing. That is to say, for a while, my extrication looked like coming off. I worked hard, ideas came, I worked hard at the ideas. I made chairs, sold them all and made a small name for myself. But as soon as things started to go right, things started to go wrong. 'Your struggling days are over,' Pa said, hugging me like a goalscorer when he heard the good news about the exhibition. 'You're getting there, son. Now you've got some light at the end of the tunnel.' This immediately made me feel uneasy: the whole point of the exercise was to stay in the tunnel, in my burrow of activity. A day or two later, I received an enigmatic telephone call. 'Put on a jacket and tie,' my father said. 'I'm picking you up in fifteen minutes.'

'What for?'

'Just get dressed,' Pa said.

I did as I was told and put on the outfit Merv's tailor had made for me. It didn't fit, but it was the only suit I had.

In the car, Pa said, 'Johnny, I'm taking you to see a friend of mine – an adviser. I'd like you to listen to what he has got to say. Just hear him out, that's all I'm asking.'

'Who is this guy?' I said.

'Mr O'Reilly,' Pa said.

'Who's Mr O'Reilly?'

The pensions and insurance man, that was who. The last person in the world I needed to see. But fifteen minutes later, there I was with my father at the office of the man to whom he had entrusted the best part of his income. O'Reilly worked high up in the Wilson Tower, the tallest skyscraper in the city, its transcendent bulk edged with blinking lights to warn off aircraft. Those beacons were redundant when Pa and I arrived there when the huge dusk sun reflected on the Tower's steel-and-glass flanks lighting the building like a blaze. Inside, though, all was cool and regulated, and when the *bing* of the elevator sounded and we were delivered into the air-conditioned chill of the thirty-first floor, it felt like we were aboard a jet plane, as though the Tower gathered momentum as it gained altitude until, at a crisis in its ascent, it took flight.

Before us was an enormous open-plan working-space where all the men, without exception, wore creaseless white shirts, dark ties and dark trousers and sat behind glossy black desks. O'Reilly was no different. The moment he saw us he leapt to his feet and gave me a firm handshake. 'How are you, John? Tommy O'Reilly.' He was about thirty-five years old. His hair was slicked back in long gleaming furrows. 'Let me get you some coffee,' he offered smilingly. 'Please, sit down.'

Pa and I sat down. He winked at me. I imagine he thought that, like him, I was nervous. 'Look around you,' Pa whispered, peering furtively about him. 'Drink it all in.'

After a delay, O'Reilly returned with three coffees. He fell into his leather swivel chair and smiled at me like an old pal.

Then, pulling out a sheaf of papers from a drawer, he said, Let's just complete this questionnaire before we do anything else. For the next ten minutes we filled out those papers question by question, box by box, with O'Reilly making simple personal enquiries in a quiet voice and transcribing the information I gave him in a slow, soothing, methodical hand. It was so relaxing that, by the end, I was on the point of sleep. Then he put the sheets away and took a sip from his coffee. Mock horror in his voice, he said, 'John, don't tell me you're not interested in a pension?'

I wanted to please O'Reilly for the patient interest he had shown in me. I smiled at his joke and made an equivocal movement with my hands.

'Pensions are for old guys, right?' O'Reilly was still spinning around in his chair, handling his coffee. 'Financial planning – that's for guys with big bucks, right?'

Again, I made a noncommittal, open-minded movement. 'I don't really know much about it,' I said.

O'Reilly put down his coffee, plucked a fresh black biro from the special thicket of black biros at his elbow and started drawing and writing as he talked. 'Then, John, with due respect, you're what we call an *uninformed client*. This firm does not do business with any person unless he or she has been properly informed. We do not wish to take advantage of anyone or push anyone into something they don't understand. What I'll do today, then, is simply give you some information.' He looked up at me, his scribbling finished. 'Once you've had a chance to think about it, you may want to come back and talk to me further. But take a look at this. This goes to the question you must have in your mind right now: why even think about financial planning?'

Bringing his paper with him, O'Reilly got up from his chair and sat right next to me on my left, shoulder to shoulder. On my right side, Pa put on his glasses and craned over to see what was going on.

The paper was headed JOHN BREEZE. On it was drawn a line, a line which was regularly intersected with vertical ticks, respectively marked, from left to right, with the numbers 0, 10,

20, 30, 40, 50, 60, 70 and 80. Each space between the ticks – an inch or so – represented a decade of my life.

'OK,' O'Reilly said. 'This is you now.' He marked the mid-twenties spot. 'No worries, no responsibilities. Right now, you're concentrating on developing your chair-making business. And that's how it should be,' O'Reilly said benevolently. 'But let's look a little further down the road, shall we? OK. John, you want kids, a family, right?'

'Well, yes,' I said automatically. 'I suppose I do. Yes.'

'And somewhere to live?'

I nodded dumbly.

With hypnotizing carefulness, O'Reilly drew two minuscule children and a box-like house. They hovered stupidly over my thirties. Then he drew an arrow from 30 to 50. 'That's twenty years of responsibility, Johnny. Minimum. Twenty years of shelling out – even if you don't want to have your children privately educated. Gene, am I right?'

Pa gave a strange intoxicated chortle. 'You certainly are.'

O'Reilly said, 'What about you, John? Anything you disagree with there?'

I shook my head.

'Right. Now, you're not going to work for ever, are you? When do you want to retire? Around sixty? Sixty-two? Let's call it sixty.' He drew an old man with a stick at the 60 mark and then grinned, mock apologetically, at Pa. 'What are you going to live off? You're self-employed, right? Well, that means you're going to have to *make provision* for these eventualities.' He gave me a friendly smile. 'You understand what I'm saying?'

I nodded.

As an afterthought joke, O'Reilly sketched a coffin at the end of the line. 'There's no need to provide for that – at least, not yet.' He winked.

I smiled back, but already I had stopped listening. Like a sucker punch, that diagram had caught me unawares. There it was, the long and the short of my life, reduced to an ineluctable line eight inches across the page. The A to Z of John Breeze.

I can see, here, that my shock might be characterized as an

imbecility. Well, it is true, anyone can tell you that life is short and then you die. Everybody knows that. But there are degrees of knowledge, and in this instance I was in the grip of an extreme state of cognition. This was not a case of simply being apprised of a new fact; no, judging by the sudden sensory jolt I experienced, I had, like the man in the sci-fi movie, the fall guy in the silver pyjamas frozen by the beam of the nerve gun, been *zapped* – the information of my doom had hit me at some electrical, irrational, neurovascular level.

That was it. From that moment forwards – yes, I can time it that precisely – things began to go downhill. The panics returned. Worst of all, it made no difference whether Angela lay with me or not and whether I stuck to her like a mollusc to rock. Even she, even love, was not enough.

I stopped functioning. When my faulty tripods came back from the workshop, I could not bring myself to fix them. Day after day I went down into the basement and day after day, I just sat there on the box, smoking cigarette after cigarette.

I have tried to speak to Angela about it – in a roundabout way. 'What's the point?' I have said. 'Who needs these things? Who cares whether I make them or not? The world is full of chairs. The last thing anybody needs is yet another place to sit down.'

'Stop feeling sorry for yourself,' Angela said.

'I'm not feeling sorry for myself,' I argued. 'I'm being honest. Whether I finish these chairs or don't finish them won't make a scrap of difference to anything. I go down there and I feel totally superfluous. I feel like nothing, like I'm disappearing from the face of the universe.' Angela laughed. 'I'm being serious,' I said. 'That's what I feel. If you're so much as a minute late for work, all hell breaks loose. If I decided never to chop another piece of wood again, no one would give a damn. I'm telling you, it scares the shit out of me.'

'My God, you've become so self-obsessed, so self-indulgent. It's not attractive, you know.'

Not attractive? What the hell did that have to do with it?

Angela said, exaggerated patience in her voice, 'Johnny, I know what you're thinking: everything is meaningless. Well, you're right. Management consultancy is meaningless, farming is meaningless, running a railway is meaningless. So what? I mean, what are you going to do about it? You have to accept it and get on with it.'

'Why should I accept it?' I said. 'Where does it say that I have to accept it?'

'Because what else are you going to do? Spend the rest of your life with that miserable look on your face?' She kneeled down on to the floor to pick up some papers. 'Johnny, a part of me doesn't believe that we're having this conversation. This is all so *basic*.'

I began to get angry. 'Basic? What are you suggesting, that I'm stupid to think about these things? You think that this is a question of intelligence?'

Angela looked at me. 'No, not intelligence. Maturity, maybe.'

'Well, that's just fine. I'm immature. And so were Shakespeare and Plato and anybody else who ever asked himself what the hell it's all about. They were just immature. They should have kept their thoughts to themselves.'

Angela came over to me, laughing. 'Don't get upset now, darling. You should hear yourself.'

I pushed her away from me. 'I'm sorry, but this isn't funny. Just because I've got the guts to take on board that we're going to die – that's right, Angela, even you're going to die, you're going to end up something that a Hoover could suck up – you think I'm some kind of a jerk.'

It was Angela's turn to lose her temper. 'Do you think you're the only one with this problem? Don't you think that we've all got to face up to the same thing?'

'Face it? The only thing you ever face are those fucking files you're always reading.'

A silence fell.

'I'm sorry,' I said eventually. 'I don't know why I said that. I'm sorry.'

Angela went back to organizing her papers. 'John, don't worry,' she said with a sigh. 'I can understand. You've lost your mother.'

I shouted, 'This has nothing to do with my mother.'

She came to me. I was trembling. She came over to me and

held me in a tight, continuing hug. I was scared, but I didn't say anything. I know, she said. She kept squeezing me. I still didn't say anything, but nevertheless Angela said, I know.

9

I miss her. I wish she were here right now.

We'd be lying down together on the sofa with a blanket pulled over us. We'd be lying there thankful for each other's simple existence. That's not sentimentality, that's a fact. Or we would be passing the time in some other way – joking around with cards, maybe, or working out a crossword. Something simple. Over there on the table, for example, is the one-thousand-piece jigsaw it took us a fortnight to finish. That scene from New England in the fall has lain there for a year, serving as a table mat. Angela did the sky, assiduously fitting the pale blue pieces at the top and the marginally less pale blues below, whereas I concentrated on the trees, thousands of fiendishly jumbled golds and reds. Then there was the toughest part, which we did together, the ground covered with fallen leaves, leaves of every possible kind of yellow.

Maybe I should get us another jigsaw. Yes, I think that's what I'll do. I'll go out tomorrow and get us another one, a real monster with nothing but sky and sky-reflecting water. It's time we did another one.

Apart from anything else, it'll do me good. That's just what I need after all that time in the cellar, some kind of occupational therapy. I've been going bananas down there. I've killed the best part of the last month manipulating a board known as the Master Maze, spending hours dribbling a small silver ball through a labyrinth punctured by one hundred holes. I became hooked, and even once I mastered the technique of effortlessly reaching the safety zone at the centre of the board, I kept playing like a moron, setting myself the goal of reversing the ball from the maze's heart right back to the starting point.

That hasn't been the worst of it. There was that period when, still clammy from the fear of the night before, I dedicated a large part of the day to obsessively quantifying my remaining lifetime. Pa was my yardstick. Thus I would take his age, fifty-six, and calculate that there were still thirty years before I reached it. Thirty years, I reminded myself, was four years more than the entirety of my life to date. That wasn't too bad, was it? But then I would work out that, aged twenty-six, probably a third of my life had already passed, and that in ten years' time – ten years being a mere five-thirteenths of my life already lived, being merely the years that had flicked past since the time I was sixteen years old, a time which felt like yesterday! – I would probably have used up *half of my total existence allotment*! In just ten years from now! I also realized that my age was *catching up* with Pa's in terms of the latter's divisibility by the former: whereas, not so long ago, at the age of twenty, I had been a mere two-fifths of my father's age, four years hence I would be only half as young as him. And then this question arose: what about Pa? How long did old Pa have to go – before he was under the ground, alone and cold?

Pa! My Pa!

It's not right. I can just see him, innocently sweating in the garden in his V-neck pullover and his beige self-belt trousers. 'I wonder what she's up to now,' he is saying. He is hoeing the soil where the rose-bushes are planted. 'This is what she loved to do when she could get a minute to herself, away from you kids. You were a handful, I can tell you.' He sinks the hoe into the ground and turns the earth. Worms appear. 'This was hers. This was where she found herself, when she worked the garden. And I mean work. Those weeds didn't stand a chance once she'd pulled her boots on, and her hat (remember her hat?). It was a massacre.' He picks up a pair of old shears and snaps at the border of the lawn. His breath is short. 'If she could see the garden now . . .' He rises from his stoop and points at a bush with the shears. 'See that? Your mother planted that.' Then he looks upwards in the mild spring sunshine. 'I'll bet you anything she's looking down and wishing she could be here.' He sweeps his eyes around the garden, then suddenly kneels by a patch of sprouting grass he has spotted. 'I'd better take care of this,' he says, clacking the shears, 'or she'll give me hell.'

I thank my stars that this is one area where he and I definitely differ: death. Just about the one worry he does not have is that of meeting his Maker. For Pa that phrase is literal – he really does believe that when he dies he will, God permitting, encounter the Man Upstairs Himself. In his belief, not only will he meet up with the Lord, but he will also run into his parents, his old buddies and, best of all, Ma. Pa looks forward to the time he will be reunited with his wife and his marriage will resume from where it left off and these years of separation will come to an end. He anticipates that day with the certainty of a man in the night anticipating the dawn. Which is great; it's wonderful he has this consolation. The snag is that, however talented he may be at scheduling railway timetables and fixing points failures, Eugene Breeze is not the country's foremost theologian.

I discovered this early on, in the course of my preparation for my first communion. One Sunday, due to the absence of the regular teacher, Pa volunteered to take the CCD class I attended after each mass and to undertake our sacramental instruction for that day. The subject under discussion, I remember, was the parable of the house built on rock and the house built on sand. The illustrated children's booklet showed it all. Two men decided to build houses for themselves. The first man – a hippie with smooth cheeks and long, curling hair – quickly put up a rickety shack on the beach which rested precariously on stilts. While the hippie strung up bring lights on his bamboo balcony and partied the nights away, the second man – a serious fellow with a dark beard and a steady gaze – unceasingly swung a pickaxe on an unpromising pile of rock, digging foundations and laying bricks until, slowly but surely, a sturdy detached home took shape there. So there you had it, one house built on sand and the other on rock, and even the class dunce knew what was going to happen next. We turned the page and, sure enough, up blew a storm, up curled a giant angry blue wave and down went the beach-house.

'What do we learn from this?' Pa asked us.

There was a silence. We knew that this was a parable and therefore that the story was not about what it seemed to be about, namely the importance of location and materials in the construction of houses. But that was all we knew. Also, I think that the story had frightened us a little bit. The last drawing showed the hippie lying on the beach next to his wrecked house, and we could not tell if he had pulled through or not. Eventually a seven-year-old arm went up. 'You have to do things properly,' someone said.

'That's right,' Pa said encouragingly. He waited a while longer for another interpretation, tossing a piece of chalk in his hand. Then he said, 'But let me tell you something else this story says. It says that if you believe in God, God will be like a rock in your life. He'll always be there with you.'

This was met with another silence. Then a girl said, 'But why shouldn't we believe in God?'

This only threw Pa for a moment. 'Well, Deirdre, some people don't believe in God. But they're wrong, because God is real. He sent Jesus, his only son, down to the world to show us how much he loved us.'

'What about people who don't believe in God, like the savages?' Deirdre said. 'Do they go to hell?'

Pa smiled. 'No, God looks after them as well. God loves the whole world.'

Then Deirdre said what we were all thinking. 'I don't understand. What about him?' She jabbed her finger at the unconscious figure stretched out on the beach.

This question clean-bowled Pa. I remember him mumbling something, but whatever he said was not an answer, and to this day the problem of evil has Pa defeated; thus whenever news of suffering innocents hits our screens, he looks on in a distressed confusion, muttering to himself. There but for the grace of God go we, I hear him whispering as we watch footage of an earthquake in central India where over a hundred thousand people dreamlessly lie in the rubble of their homes. This, remember, from a man fully insured against Acts of God.

To be fair, I do not blame Pa for his failure to crack these puzzles. Why should he have a watertight theory of everything? After all, who the hell is he? Just another human being who gets up in the morning and does his best to get through the day without mishap. Like everybody else, he leaves the business of ontological breakthroughs to the specialists, relying on any developments to filter down through the usual channels. Good news travels. Look at the Gospel. A few fishermen – correction, a few writers who borrowed their names – record pure hearsay concerning a long-gone woodworker and before you know it, on the strength of evidence that wouldn't stand up a second in any half-decent court, the whole world has latched on to it. Even now, two thousand years later, a huge infrastructure is still in place to broadcast these same glad, unreal tidings. You can't turn a corner in Rockport without running into a church. So who can blame Pa for falling into line on religion and leaving the fine detail of it to the experts?

The problem, though, comes when you actually scrutinize these experts in action. Just the other day, for example, I came across a theological debate in the newspaper which was literally a scandal – a stumbling-block to faith.

The subject of the argument was the efficacy of prayer. The first writer, an Anglican bishop I believe, stated that prayer had no power to alter the relationship between the beneficiary of the prayer and the real world. It did, however, strengthen the relationship between the worshipper and the Lord. Thus praying for the success of your child in his or her exams would confer a spiritual benefit upon you, but would not help your child. The Lord did not give preferential treatment to examinees lucky enough to have people requesting His intercession.

This theory, with its implicit admission that God is at best a concerned bystander, was depressing enough, but at least it made sense. The next theory – by a Roman Catholic bishop, a leader of my own church – was not merely disheartening, it was ludicrous. He said this: that a prayer for good exam results would be efficacious *even if you were standing there with the results letter unopened in your hand*. The reasoning: that since the Lord's omniscience extended to a knowledge of the future, He would have known about your last-minute, too-late prayer in advance and would therefore have interceded *before the prayer was made*!

What really got me down was the glee with which the prelate expounded this exquisite absurdity. It was clear, from the note of exclamation and grinning triumph upon which his argument ended, that he felt it possessed an ingenuity and logic that made it truly irresistible. Even now I can see the bishop at his desk, licking the envelope addressed to the newspaper with a long, satisfied application of the tongue. That is that, he thinks. My good deed for the day.

When I think of Merv, the poor fucker! And these are the clowns we're supposed to go to for guidance!

Suddenly everything swerves, and without warning I find myself recalling an afternoon many years ago when Pa and I sat before the television watching the live broadcast of Rockport United versus Clonville in the replay of the semifinals of the FA Cup. The red United shirts are swarming forward towards the Clonville goal as the team searches for an equalizer, and in the stands fluid crowds surge and eddy like sea water trapped in a creek, the fans pouring through the crush-barriers in red and white currents each time the team comes close to scoring and then sucking back up the terraces in the aftermath of the near-miss. One-nil down and ten minutes to go! My father and I are transfixed by that game and when the sound of descending feet comes from the staircase we do not look up – how can we, when at that exact moment Mickey Lazarus is swinging over a deep cross to the leaping figure of Dean? Then, just as the header skims the bar, there is the noise of the front door shutting quietly, a click of locks, and though Pa looks up momentarily to see who it is, his attention is drawn straight back to the television, to the action replay of that last attack. There is the move all over again, Lazarus jinking left and then jinking right and then striking that high, floating ball one more time.

'He was pushed!' I shout. 'That should have been a penalty! Pa, Dean was fouled when he went for the ball!'

We hear the distant slam of a door, a car door, and Pa gets to his feet and goes to the window, all the time keeping an eye on the television, where for a last, agonizing time, Peter Dean and his marker are slowly rising together at the far post. An engine starts in the street, and just as Pa goes to open the curtains to look outside, another *ooh* rips out from the turned-up sound-box of the TV and he spins round just in time to catch Seamus Loasby, the legendary United centre forward, clean through with no one to beat but the keeper, scoop the ball over the bar and into the crowd, and just in time to miss waving goodbye to his wife as she drives off into town for the last time.

That moment, which came only months after Pa's best-ever day, Christmas Day, 1979, was probably the worst in Pa's life. It was at that moment that United blew their last chance of a big trophy; and it was at that moment, at twenty-five minutes to five on Wednesday, 16 April 1980, that Ma was lost for good. All of this on a day my father was wearing his lucky underpants.

It could happen to me. I could lose Angela just as my father lost my mother. Not literally; not lightning striking twice. But any day Angela could be gone, for good.

10

My God, she's two and a half hours late.

Anything could have happened to her. Anything.

Right that's it.

I snatch up my coat and grab the keys. Enough is enough. It's time to take matters into my own hands. It's time for action.

I catch sight of myself in the mirror. There I am, standing in the middle of the room in my coat. What do I think I'm doing? Am I going to run around the streets looking for her, asking passers-by whether they've seen a woman with long dark hair and blue eyes? Am I going to shout her name down alley-ways? Whistle? This is Angela we're talking about, not Trusty.

I pocket the keys. I have to be calm, calm and methodical. I have to think. Where is she most likely to be?

I go to the telephone and punch some numbers.

No answer at her parents' home.

Her office. I'll ring up her office.

I dial the number, panting slightly.

No reply. Nobody at the switchboard.

I ring again, to make sure.

Still no reply.

Damn. Damn.

I know: I'll telephone the flat. It's a long shot, but maybe Rosie will be able to tell me something. Maybe she'll have received a message. You never know.

Rosie picks up the telephone immediately, with a gasped 'Hello?'

'It's me,' I say. She is silent – and I remember that Steve, too, is absent.

'I don't know what to do,' Rosie says. 'He's been gone for hours.'

I move the telephone to my mouth, but I say nothing. This is not the moment to ask about Angela.

'I'm going to kill him when he gets back,' Rosie swears. 'I'm going to . . . I'm going to . . .'

She abandons the sentence, her vocabulary of vengeance failing her, but she's said enough to make me nervous. With her track record – the smashed plates, the hurled dictionaries, the slapped faces, the upturned tables – Rosie's threats of violence have a certain credibility. Look at what happened on Tuesday night. I was trying to watch television when I became aware that a fight was going on, which means that I became aware of Rosie shouting at Steve. I turned up the sound of the TV and tried to ignore it. This didn't work, because whatever the fracas was about, it involved a lot of running in and out of the room and a lot of slamming of doors. As far as I could make out, the altercation was following the usual pattern: initial bust-up in the sitting-room; muffled reconciliations in the bedroom; twenty-minute silence; half-time break as Steve padded out to make two cups of tea; fresh losses of temper; raised voices; and another showdown in front of me in the sitting-room. The same old farce they went through, and put me through, night after night.

Eventually there arrived a lengthy lull and it seemed as if at last things had been patched up. Steve emerged from the bedroom to go to the lavatory and Rosie came into the room and asked for a cigarette. She stood there for a moment, smoking calmly, and did not react when the flushing sound came and went from the bathroom. Steve returned, still tucking his shirt into his trousers. He gave me an apologetic grin. Rosie swivelled and silently, with a full swing of the leg, brought the toe of her shoe hard against his shin. The crack of the bone sounded above the volume of the television. Crying out, Steve grabbed his injured leg and took three or four sidewards hops on the other leg, trying to keep his balance. He failed. He fell over, the back of his head catching the door-edge with another crack. Before I could react, Rosie was standing over him kicking him again and again while he lay curled on the ground moaning, grunting like a tennis player bashing a groundstroke each time she made contact with her foot.

'Rosie! For fuck's sake!' I shouted.

I jumped up to stop her but by this time she was already

down on her knees next to Steve and sobbing ashamedly, Sorry, sorry, sorry . . .

Christ, it makes me sweat just thinking about it. So I say into the telephone, 'Rosie, calm down, all right? Don't get angry with him. He's just gone out, that's all. He'll be back.'

But then my anxiety about Rosie's death threats wanes a little, because I remember that for a long, long time now there has been a chasm between Rosie's promised actions and her actual ones. *I'm going to . . .* How many times have we heard that phrase from her over the years? 'I'm going to quit that job tomorrow,' she vows almost every time she returns from a hard day at work. 'I'm going to go to Mrs Freely and hand in my notice.' Her cigarette catches fire, the lighter lid snaps down hard beneath her thumb, the flame is engulfed. 'I hate it, I hate it, I hate it. It's all so disgusting, everything about it makes me feel sick – the passengers, the food, the pilots, the stewards, the girls, these clothes . . .' She makes a gesture of revulsion at her uniform. 'One of these days I'm going to . . . I'm going to . . .' She sucks at her cigarette, plotting. 'Yes, I'll show them.'

I'm going to . . . It could be Rosie's motto. 'At the end of this week I'm going to tell Steve to pack his bags.' Or, when Pa is about to pay us a visit, 'I'm going to cook us all a nice meal: steaks, salad, vegetables, the works. I'll get some good fillet steaks. I'm going to spoil him, the poor thing; he's working much too hard.' Those are another couple of *I'm going tos* which have yet to reach fruition. Yes, even my sister's best intentions, of which, at one time, there used to be plenty, have not come good. Poor Rosie! For her whole adult life she has teetered between potentialities and their realization. When she left university in her early twenties, nobody doubted that Rosemary Breeze would feast on life's dangling fruit. With the long reach which her brains and her beauty afforded her, success and happiness would be easy pickings. But it just never happened. Her first scheme was to go abroad for a year, but that did not really come off because the waitressing job she took to raise the money did not pay well enough. All that her year of travel added up to was three weeks in Spain and six months at the Rockport Pizza Hut. Returning from Spain all brown and skinny and raring to go, her red hair streaked with yellow, it was *I'm going to be a teacher*. When, during the year of professional training, she discovered that the work disagreed with her, she took a temporary job, again as a waitress. It was around this time, when she was twenty-three, that Steve made his appearance. He was temporary, too, according to Rosie. A plaything for the summer, nothing more. I'm going to have some fun for a while, she said defensively. It isn't for ever. (Temporary: who can blame her for wanting temporary? Who wants finality?) Soon afterwards, Rosie fell out with her flatmate and, as an interim measure, moved in to Steve's place in that tower block. For a year or two Pa and I hardly saw her. During this time the waitressing job ended – we were never told how or why – and for a long time, for over a year, Rosie did not go back to work. When asked by Pa about getting a job, any job, out it came, *I'm going to*, the phrase used for the first time by way of postponement and not anticipation. Then Pa bought the flat. 'A fresh start,' he said. Shortly after, Rosie joined the airline: *I'm just going to do this while I look for something else*. A stopgap, that was the thinking. Wishful thinking, because Rosie has not, so far as I am aware, got round to job-hunting. It is not surprising. Five years ago, yes, you could understand her ambition and believe in it. But since that time – this is a terrible thing to say, but it is true – Rosie has gone into a decline. Her nerves, her stamina, her sociability, even her intelligence: they are not what they were. So much so that, far from quitting her job, Rosie will do well to hold on to it. At twenty-eight, she is still teetering, except now it is no longer on the rim of success, but on a brink. My sister is toeing a sheer drop.

Pa can't bear it. 'Why did she do it, Johnny?' he asked. (This was yesterday, on our way back from the hospital.) 'Why did she do it?' He turned the car around a corner.

I didn't have the strength to say anything. Seeing Merv had wiped me out.

Pa said, 'It's a crime. It's a crime when you've hair that long and beautiful to just chop it all off.' He took a right. 'Where will it end?'

'He's seeing another woman,' Rosie says. She cries out, 'The shit! The shit!'

'Come on, Rosie,' I say, 'don't get all worked up. You know that's not true. Steve would never do anything like that.'

'You don't know him,' Rosie says. She sniffs. 'And I've been so horrible to him,' she says with a trembling voice.

I automatically begin to take issue with her, in order to comfort her, but then I stop. She *has* been horrible to Steve.

Rosie starts crying. 'My hair,' she says. 'That's what did it. My hair.'

I feel awful for her. 'Rosie,' I say.

Rosie's hair. Here is the terrible truth about it: not that cutting it was vandalism, but that it was not. The fact is, Rosie was beginning to look a little absurd with that girlish, overlong fleece.

'Johnny,' she says, 'what am I going to do?'

There is nothing Rosie can do. 'Just wait,' I say. 'Don't worry, he'll be back.' There is a pause. 'Just be nice to him when he gets back, all right?'

There is a desperate silence.

'Rosie?'

'He's seeing someone else,' she says finally. 'I know he is. I don't know what I'm going to do if I lose him,' she says. She hangs up.

I'm very tired and I have to sit down. I fish out a crooked cigarette from its packet. Angela, I think.

Then I think, Losing Steve: is it possible? Mislaying Mr Stay-Put himself? I suppose if anybody could manage it, it is Rosie. She could squander just about anything. Her beauty, for example. Her marvellous idiosyncratic looks are leaving her, moving on to settle down on other faces. When I see the sparkle of my sister's blue-green eyes, it is not in her face but in the girl's at the supermarket check-out; her smooth cheekbones now belong to the woman at the travel agency; and now the redhead turning heads in the street is somebody else. Of course, nobody keeps their looks for ever, but Rosie seems to be discarding hers, trashing them before their time in the way that, in her cleaning frenzies, she throws away half-full cartons of milk and newly opened jam-jars. Her hair needed to be cut, yes, but not savaged like that. She smokes, she cakes her face every morning in a thick muck of make-up, she constantly eats junk food, she takes no exercise. Of course, there would be nothing wrong with all of this self-neglect if it did not bother her. But it does. She inspects herself in the morning and says, 'Wrinkles. More wrinkles every day.' And it's true, there they are, fanning out from the edges of her oval eyes at the slightest move of her face. Her voice grows hoarse. 'One year. I've got one more year. Then that'll be it. It'll be over. And look at these open pores,' she wails, pointing at microscopic apertures under her eyes. 'Look at them. They're everywhere. I've got a face like a dartboard!' She laughs at the simile – we all laugh, because it's a good one – and then begins to weep. I would like to hug her tightly at this point, to take her in my arms and secure her with a brother's love.

And then there is Pa. With her constant unkindness to him, Rosie is doing her best to lose him, too. Of course, that could never happen. Pa's love is unlosable. Pa still believes in his daughter no matter what, believes that, like Steve, she has inner resources. 'She doesn't mean it,' he tells me after she has hurt him again with some remark. 'She has a heart of gold,' he says, and I stupidly imagine a lump of that soft metal implanted in my sister's breast.

A heart of gold: I suppose it's no surprise that Pa should resort to platitudes like this. That's how he often deals with difficulties, by grasping on to tried and tested sayings as though they were the warm rungs of wisdom's ladder. Right now, I'll bet, he is lying in bed and telling himself that it is darkest before the dawn and that all clouds have silver linings. He is saying to himself that although, one, his best friend is in intensive care; two, his job is at risk; three, his children are sources of fear and anxiety; four, he has been attacked by a strange man and by a dog; five, his refereeing hobby is a humiliation; six, his pet is missing; seven, his house has been broken into and the precious photographs of his late wife, herself robbed from him, have been stolen, although all of these things are true, at least he and his children are healthy, at least his house is intact – *things could be worse*, Pa is saying to himself.

Now this relativism may be true (although, in fact, things *are* worse: Pa still does not know about the imminent collapse of my exhibition, does he?), but surely even Pa knows that it is also crap. Everybody knows that.

Pa's fondness for adages has spilled over into his work. Prompted by the arrival of Paddy Browne, the Network whizz-kid, he has taken to reading executive success books, in particular the *How To* books written by a management guru called Mark Q. Fincham: *The How To of Negotiation, The How To of Team Play* and *The How To of Making Contacts.* Every chapter in a Mark Q. Fincham book begins with a pithy epigraph in glittering italics and it is these, rather than the body of the work, which really impress my father. 'How about this,' he says. '*Build your adversary a golden bridge to retreat across.* Sun Tzu.' He leafs through some more pages. '*In the long run, men only hit what they aim at.* Henry David Thoreau.' He is full of admiration. 'You should read this, John. There's some great stuff here. *Nobody shoulders a rifle in defence of a boarding house.* Bret Harte. Now that's smart.' He reads on. '*Success as an executive requires the presence of many qualities – whereas failure will proceed from the absence of merely one of them.*' Pa hesitates over this one. He starts to say something but then stops. Then he says defensively, 'Dr Robert N. McMurry. Who the hell is he, anyway?'

His favourite business Bible is Fincham's *What They Don't Teach You at Rockport Business School,* because Paddy Browne went to Rockport Business School and Pa figures that reading this book will give him some kind of edge over the man. Following Fincham's recommendation, he carries around in his wallet the special takeaway cards that come with the books, cards which boil the techniques of business down to their mysterious essence. DIAGNOSIS, one card reads. NON-POSTPONEMENT, reads another one. INPUT? THROUGHPUT? OUTPUT? asks another. And my favourite: INEVITABLE PROBLEMS – QUICK RESPONSE. It's the dash I love – that immediate, right-on-top-of-the-problem dash.

Answer me this: Merv's accident – what is the quick response to that?

11

Merv is being treated in a hospital just outside Rockport city. It is an isolated, dark-bricked, turreted old building and for panoramic reasons, one supposes, its founders located it right on the precipice that overshadows the Rockport yacht haven, giving the place the bleak, looming air of a Central European schloss. We approached it by a narrow road that ran alongside the edge of the cliff. Below, to our right, was the city in its basin and, to our left, on the exposed flatland in front of the hospital, stood a wind farm, the propellers planted in the arid earth in parallel rows, blades spinning sweetly in the plentiful sea wind.

We arrived just after three o'clock. There was a moment of quiet after the car stopped. An ambulance drew up to the hospital entrance, its roof light turning orange again and again. Neither of us felt like moving.

Pa tapped me on the shoulder. 'Look,' he said, pointing. I looked: way below, a train, slithering carefully through gardens and allotments into North Rockport Station. Pa checked his watch. 'Bang on time,' he said.

We got out of the car and walked into the reception area and Pa asked about seeing Mr Mervyn Rasmussen in intensive care. First floor, take a right, take a left, go down to the bottom of the corridor, the receptionist said, then wait in the waiting-room.

'Hold on a moment,' Pa said, just as we were about to set off. He dashed outside and came back moments later with a bouquet of daffodils and a get-well card with a joke. *It could be worse,* the front of the card said. I looked inside it for the punchline: *I could be ill and you could be listening to me complaining!*

BEST WISHES FOR A SPEEDY RECOVERY, MERV, Pa wrote. WITH BEST WISHES FROM THE BREEZES. He signed his name and Rosie's, and then I signed. 'OK,' he said worriedly. 'I suppose we'd better get going.'

We walked without speaking. We turned one corner, then another. Finally, after what seemed like half an hour going down a long corridor, we reached the intensive care waiting-room. It felt like an airport lounge full of delayed passengers. The atmosphere was one of exhaustion and camaraderie and domestic informality, the visitors unkempt, walking around in socks, eating snacks, dipping into bags for belongings. A television was on in the corner. There was a low hum of conversation.

Pa said, 'There she is. That's Mrs Rasmussen – Amy. And that's Merv's boy,' he whispered. 'He's called Billy.' We approached them. 'Amy,' Pa said. He gave her a big hug while Billy and I stood awkwardly by.

'Billy,' Mrs Rasmussen said, 'you remember Mr Breeze?' Pa and Billy shook hands. 'And you must be John,' Mrs Rasmussen said. We shook hands. Then, after a moment of hesitation, Billy Rasmussen and I shook hands, too. Billy was a big-shouldered, brown-skinned man of about my age. His hands were enormous. He kept half grinning, as if there were something comical about the situation.

Mrs Rasmussen was a tiny Oriental woman of around fifty, a Filipino by origin, I guessed. She was wearing a pyjama suit and slippers and obviously had been camping out in the waiting-room since the accident. I could see a sleeping-bag and a small suitcase under her chair.

'How is he, Amy?' Pa said.

Mrs Rasmussen shrugged. 'Not good, Gene.'

Pa went quiet for a moment. He made to hold up the daffodils, but then he lowered them again.

Mrs Rasmussen said kindly, 'You don't have to see him, you know. You can leave the flowers with me, if you like.'

Pa moved a little.

'Would you like to see him?' Mrs Rasmussen said. She looked at me.

Pa said. 'Only if it's OK, Amy. We don't want to disturb him.'

Mrs Rasmussen smiled. Her tiredness showed. 'Of course

it's all right. You're his best friend.' Then she smiled at me, as if I, too, were a best friend of Merv.

A nurse nodded his approval to Mrs Rasmussen and we followed her through one door and then through another, her slippers slapping against her heels. She pointed through a third transparent door. 'He's in there,' she said. 'I'll wait here,' she said.

Looking uncertainly through the door-glass, Pa went in. Not wanting to wait outside with Mrs Rasmussen, I followed him.

Almost immediately I broke out into a sweat. The ward was fervid as a jungle. On the bed in front of us a fat, bright red naked body, the skin lacquered with cream, lay wrapped in transparent plastic sheeting. That was not Merv. Merv was a pale, skinny man. We had no business with this fat man. We quickly walked past to the second bed, the one behind the screen.

Pa and I looked at each other. The bed was empty.

Pa undid his collar and took off his coat. He said with a weak smile, 'Boy, I tell you, I could grow some plants in here, that's for sure.'

I said, pointing back towards the first bed, 'That . . . That isn't him, is it?'

Pa fanned his face with the greeting-card and looked at me anxiously.

We went back. Pa slowly approached the unconscious patient and leaned over him.

'Well?' I said, after a moment.

'I . . . I'm not sure.'

I was. That was not Merv. Merv was spindly. This poor guy was shaped like the blow-up Michelin man, all puffy and creased. His face was round as a football and his eyes were slits, whereas Merv had a thin face and big eyes; and although it was hard to be sure, because he was lying on his bed, I saw no sign of a hump. Besides, I had an idea about what we were looking for: a man with the appearance of a physics experiment, encased in bandages and plaster, with his arms and legs suspended by weights and pulleys from the ceiling.

Then Pa said, 'It's Merv. He's been burned.'

I moved forward.

look at photographs, something does come back. But that's it. The laughs, the looks, the moments, the company, the fun, the reality of her, her thereness – all gone. For good. This is what I cannot get away from any more at night, this is what leaves me sweating and sleepless and outraged: *for good*. It happened last night and it's happening now, this crushing realization: soon it will all be over, *for good. In perpetuity.*

No. No.

Another cigarette, quick.

Calm yourself, Johnny, calm yourself. It will not matter, death is not an experience, and besides, the eternity that preceded you wasn't so bad, was it? So why mind the one in store? You don't pity the dead, so stop pitying yourself. Grow up. It happens to everybody. It's natural, everything ends.

But I reject that! That is cowardice, not maturity! I am John Breeze, I am alive, I refuse to disappear!

But I will.

Here they come again, all together: disbelief, certainty and freezing fear.

All of a sudden it is as though I am floating. Although I am standing with both feet solidly on the floor, my legs may as well be hanging in thin air. I recognize the feeling. It is that of the boy suspended high up on the seat of a see-saw as three others sit on the grounded seat, outweighing the boy and keeping him up there in the sky against his will. He shakes at the handlebar and kicks his legs, but nothing is changed and he remains where he is, powerless and dangling. A double fear preys on the boy's mind: the fear of remaining airborne indefinitely and the fear of the alternative, the letdown, the crunching drop to earth. Either way, he is helpless and this, in the end, is perhaps the worst, most distressing thing: he is wholly at the mercy of the three others. They know this, and this is the kick they get out of it. They are in charge. The imbalance favours them spectacularly. They are reddening and squealing with the purity of the thrill.

It's frightening; I feel so afloat, so unreal, that I could be in a dream. But I'm here, God damn it, I'm here in the flesh!

I take off my jumper and go to the kitchen to run cold water against my face. Maybe there is something wrong with my metabolism, or my blood circulation. Maybe the central heating is turned up too high.

I return to the living-room and just move around for a few moments. Then decisively I leap up and catch hold of the solid rim of the bed and hang there like an ape for a few moments until the muscles in my shoulders and arms ache with the weight of my body. I keep hanging there, letting the pain worsen until I'm fighting to hold my grip. Then I let go and land.

I feel a little more awakened. OK, that's a bit better. Now let's put some music on and maybe try another cigarette.

There's an old Beatles album on the turntable. That'll do.

A song or two go by and then on it comes, 'Here Comes the Sun', George Harrison, and I remember a glittering winter afternoon – was it a year or two years ago? – when this song was playing and this room shone. In the sudden confluence of the music and the light, Angela and I spontaneously looked up at each other from our Sunday newspapers and rose to our feet to hold each other in the luminous centre of the room, grinning at each other with delight, and Angela said, her eyes actually glistening, Is this heaven? Are we there?

I hit the stop button. The needle-arm floats back to its rest.

I drop face-down on to the sofa, eyes closed. My shoes fall from my feet.

But a sleepless minute later, I roll over on to my side to make myself more comfortable, and momentarily my eyes blink open again. There is the praying-chair, six feet away.

Pa asked me to pray for Merv.

I shut my eyes. Forget it, Pa. Dream on.

I roll off the sofa. I go over to the chair and remove the fern and wipe clean the ring of earth the plantpot has left on the uncushioned hassock. I kneel down, resting my elbows on the praying-desk. The wood is rock-hard on the kneecaps.

OK, God, I'm going to make this quick. Help Merv. Help him to pull through.

I shift my knees. Help Mrs Rasmussen, too, and the son, what's his name, Billy. Then I think, What the hell, and I say to God, And help Pa. Help him to get through this weekend and help him to keep his job. Keep him healthy. Help Rosie, too.

Help her to find happiness. She's in big trouble, she needs a hand, she needs every hand on deck. A pause. Help Angela. Please let her be safe. Let her come back tonight. Oh, yes, and Steve. Don't forget Steve. Keep an eye out for that poor bastard, as well. Make sure he gets back in one piece.

I stay where I am, leaning hard on the desk.

Help me, as well, God.

A feeling of surrealism overcomes me. I remember the poet who took a lobster for a walk.

Then I remember Ma, but cannot recall her. Ma, who was my mother.

I get up. I move over to the windows and part the curtains one more time. It has stopped raining. The golden shapes of windows in the houses across the street have disappeared. There is no sign of Angela. Above the rooftops, dark spaces of sky appear where the wind has ripped up the clouds.

13

'Close the door!'

The man sitting in front of me leans over and smashes shut the carriage door, killing the draught.

'I can't believe the rudeness of these people,' he says to me. He is about fifty years old. Stiff white sprigs of hair jut from his nostrils.

I raise my eyebrows mutely.

The man straightens his tie. 'Mind you, these trains don't help, do they? I mean, why don't they have electric doors which open and close automatically? Why do we have to put up with this rubbish? They've got electric doors in Holland, France, Germany – they've even got them in Italy. Why haven't we got them?'

Again, I agree with a meek movement of the face. I glance briefly at the other person in the carriage, a lady in her seventies. She has a bandage taped over her left eye.

'It's a joke,' the man says. 'A bad joke.'

'Excuse me,' the lady says. 'I wonder if you might tell me when we arrive in Waterville. You see, I can't see very well. I've had an operation.'

'Of course, madam,' the man says. 'But this is the express, you know. We're not stopping anywhere.'

'Thank you,' she says, and closes her visible eye.

The man shakes his head and picks up his newspaper, and finally I'm free to look out through the window at the slowly reversing green fields where, in the distance, a smooth cluster of racehorses hovers up a slope.

The countryside. I'm out. Rockport is behind me.

At long last. At long bloody last.

It has been some week.

When I came to on Monday morning, the curtains bright as a cinema screen, I pulled the bedspread over my head and shut my eyes. Lying there half asleep, I fantasized for a marvellous moment that if I lay there long enough and let events take their course without me, a time would finally come when my situation would be well and truly superseded and when I might step out freely into a new world apparelled in fresh circumstances, the discarded past lying crumpled in a corner like a worn shirt.

But then I woke up properly. There was no warm back against which to press myself, no soft-cheeked buttocks and smooth neck. Angela had still not returned.

I eased myself down the bed ladder and drew aside the curtains. I swung open the window, letting in the noise of the cars and the day. It was the rush hour.

I telephoned Angela's office. 'Extension 274, please.'

I was put through. A man's voice said, 'Yes?'

'Could I speak to Angela Flanagan, please?'

'Hold on,' the man said. Half a minute later, he said, 'She doesn't seem to be around at the moment. Can I take a message?'

'What, you mean she's not at work today?'

'Who is this?'

'It's a personal call,' I said.

'Look, I'm afraid I don't know where she is.'

I hesitated. 'This is her boyfriend, John Breeze,' I said. 'It's just that I'm worried about her whereabouts.'

'Her boyfriend? Angela's boyfriend?' the man said.

'That's right,' I said. I felt like a fourteen-year-old.

He said, 'I'll make a note that you rang. I'll tell her to call you, OK?'

'OK,' I said.

But where could she be?

I took a shower and got dressed in day-old clothes and went to catch a bus home. The woman sitting in front of me was reading a newspaper. ROCKPORT FANS RUN RIOT, the headline read.

I looked away. The morning, like a footballer running out for the kick-off, was freshly kitted out in a deep blue sky striped by pure trails of clouds. The chestnut trees rocked easily beneath their newly heavyweight greenery and as usual the Rockport traffic moved fluently through clean roads and neat bicycle lanes. It all looked so pleasant and harmonious and according-to-plan. Things will turn out fine, I said to myself. Things will fall into place.

Five minutes later, I opened the front door of the flat.

It had been smashed up. The remains of crockery and glass lay on the floor, stains of red liquid spattered the walls, books and magazines were scattered everywhere, my prints had been wrecked and, judging from the heap of forks and knives by the door to the kitchen, the whole cutlery drawer had been hurled to the ground.

There was no sign of Steve or Rosie.

I fell into a chair. Don't tell me we've been broken into. Please don't tell me that.

The doorbell rasped, then rasped once more.

I got to my feet and looked out to see who it was. Two big men with crew-cut hair and casual clothing stood outside, shielding their eyes from the sun as they looked up and down at the house.

Who were these people?

They rang again, insistently.

I spoke through the intercom. 'Who is it?' I said. I heard an exchange of words. 'Who is it?' I repeated.

'Mr Breeze, is it?' a man said.

After a moment, I said, 'Yes. Who is this?'

'We've come from Mr Devonshire,' the man said. 'We've come for the chairs.'

The chairs. Shit.

Instinctively I decided to bluff, lie and stall. 'Look,' I said, 'look, this isn't a good time. Could you come back later? It's just that I've got my hands full at the moment.'

'We'll only be a second, Mr Breeze.' The voice was determined. 'We'll just be in and out.'

I rested my head against the wall, trying to think. Then I buzzed open the door. To hell with it.

The men came in. 'Well,' one of them said cheerfully, 'where do we go?' He stopped to stare at the state of the living-room. 'That must have been some party,' he quipped.

'They're downstairs,' I heard myself saying. 'I'll show you.'

It was out of my hands. The men loaded the stools into their van while I stood around watching them. They slammed shut the rear doors of the van, white swinging doors like the doors of an ambulance. 'Don't worry,' the talkative one said as they climbed into the cab and his friend started up the engine. 'They're safe as houses with us.'

I gave him a thin smile. As it happened, my last remaining chance was that the chairs were not safe as houses, that by some miracle the van would crash on the way to the gallery and the stools would be destroyed in the process.

I went back inside. Fuck it. I was glad to see the back of those chairs. So what if the exhibition did not take place? It didn't matter, not when you compared it to everything else that was going on. Pa would understand. And let Devonshire sue me if he wanted to. It would be a barren exercise. I was a man of straw, with no assets to speak of, nothing upon which a judgement could be enforced.

Then I remembered. There was one asset that I did have: the flat. Pa had signed it over to me to avoid death duties. Officially, this place was mine.

I crumpled into an armchair. Not the flat. Please, not the flat, too.

And Angela, what about her?

I sat there, my limbs lifelessly dangling. Then I registered a stinging in my fingers: a cigarette, burned down to the bottom.

It was ten minutes before I was able to face things. I made an inspection of the flat. The sitting-room was the only room that had been touched and nothing appeared to be missing. So if it wasn't a break-in, what had happened? I noticed that Rosie's travelling bag was not in its usual place in the bathroom – which meant that she had gone off to work.

This wasn't the work of robbers. This was down to my demented sister. For some crazy reason she had destroyed the place she normally slaved to keep so clean.

And where was Steve? It was ten-thirty in the morning: why wasn't he in bed?

I felt a flicker of concern for the deadbeat. If Rosie had done this to the flat, God knew what she might have done to him.

Picking up a knife from the floor, I made myself toast with the one slice of stale bread left in the kitchen. I looked for some jam. No jam. Correction: there was jam, but it was in the living-room, at the foot of the far wall, lying in a sticky mass where the pot had burst. That bitch. That fucking bitch. I'd had enough of her crap. She was going to pay for this. The next time I saw her I'd . . .

I breathed deeply. I ate the buttered toast.

I decided to telephone my father at work. I wanted to know how he was after his awful weekend and how Paddy Browne's report had gone. Most of all, I wanted to hear his voice.

'Gene Breeze, please,' I said.

'What's it in connection with?' the receptionist asked. 'Is this a customer complaint?'

I said, 'No, this is John, his son.'

'Ah, right. One moment, please.'

I was put through. But the extension number rang and rang without answer.

I hung up, rang back and explained.

'Let me make enquiries,' the receptionist said. Moments later, she said, 'He's not in at the moment, John. He's at home.'

At home?

'You're sure?' I said.

'Er, yes,' the woman said. 'I . . .' She stopped. 'At least, I assume he is. He's not here, I know that.'

I rang off and dialled Pa's home number.

No answer. Where the fuck was everybody?

Brushing perspiration from my mouth, I telephoned Angela at home – nobody there – and again at work. This time somebody else from her department answered, another man, another shithead with a glib tone of voice. No, he said, Angela was still not around. Yes, he said, he'd take a message that I had called.

Who were all these characters? Were there no women in management consultancy?

I smashed down the receiver.

I became aware again of the state of the room.

I had to get out. I went out and jumped on a bus to Pa's place.

The bus climbed up to the leafy suburb where Pa lives, known as Birds' District because all of the streets are named after birds. A prickling feeling of relief came to me as the bus turned slowly through Merl Street and Crow Street and on to Bluebird Lane, scattering young boys with bats who were warming up for the cricket season. The neighbourhood was changeless. At Canary Street I rang the stopping-bell when I saw the grocer's, just as Ma had coached me to do almost twenty years ago when together we travelled on this same bus route every day for a week so that I would learn how to get to school. The bus stopped at the corner of Curlew Lane and Turtledove Lane. I jumped off heavily and slowly walked down the street, familiar with each step of the way, with every jutting paving-slab, every manhole and gas outlet, every cleanly shaped hedge. I passed the house where Mr Murphy, the anaesthetist with the home-made nuclear bunker in the garden, still lived, then the house of Dr Michaelson, the mathematics professor who played chess with Pa in the evenings over a glass of Bushmills, then the house of Mr Johnson, the schizophrenic. And then, looking ahead, I saw my father's silhouette a hundred yards away, hosing the ground in front of him with a strong jet of water. Pa! I shouted, and I waved, and he looked up and straightened, sending an arc of water into the sunlit air, and the moment that followed was a moment from an idyll, my upright father strongly waving one arm, while the other arm, perfectly still, sprayed a perfectly crayonned rainbow over the road.

He was washing dog-shit from the pavement. When I reached him I stood silently by for a moment or two, watching the accurate torrent crumbling the foul then sending it streaming down over the edge of the kerb.

The pavement cleansed and darkened, Pa turned the hose on to his car, rinsing off the dust and the massive patches of brown and white goose-crap that had exploded on the roof and front windscreen. Then he turned off the tap at the front of the house and energetically looped the green hose around it. He looked at me with his one straight eye, said, 'Come in', and marched me into the kitchen, where he began making two coffees. 'Well, son,' he said, 'you may be wondering how Paddy Browne's review meeting went today.'

I accepted the coffee he offered me and followed him into

the living-room. A toolbox and electrical equipment lay by the broken french windows. Pa got down on to his knees and started playing with a volt-meter.

'Well?' I said. 'How did it go? What did Paddy Browne have to say?'

Momentarily distracted by his work, he took a few seconds to reply. 'Browne? Browne said nothing,' he said. 'I haven't spoken to Browne.'

I looked into the garden. The pear tree in blossom there reappeared indoors, adrift in the spotless glass of the coffee table.

My father stood up and raised his eye-patch to his forehead in order better to examine the volt-meter. 'Johnny, there was no review meeting. They fired me.'

I said, 'What?'

'They canned me, son. They gave me the bullet. Hold this,' he said, passing me a Philips screwdriver. He looked up and saw my face. He laughed. 'Don't look so shocked, boy. It happens, you know.'

'But, Pa,' I said, 'I don't understand. They can't do this, not after all your years of service.'

'Well, Johnny, they just did.' He concentrated on inserting a screw into the windowframe. 'Fifteen minutes. They gave me fifteen minutes to clear my desk. I give them twenty-six years and they give me quarter of an hour.' He reached up and took back the screwdriver.

I could not believe it; most of all, I could not believe how robustly Pa, who only last night had been unable to climb out of his own bath, was taking it. 'What are you going to do?' I said.

'You know who else they sacked?' Pa said, standing up. 'Merv. They sacked Merv.' He wiped his face. 'They're going to pay for this,' he said. 'I haven't been in this business for a quarter of a century for nothing. I know my rights, and I'm going to sue them. Unfair dismissal,' Pa said. 'I wasn't consulted,' he said, pointing his screwdriver at his heart. 'Nobody asked me anything – me, a man of my seniority. No warning, no nothing. They just went ahead and fired me like a nobody.'

I shook my head. 'That's terrible,' I said.

'It isn't right, Johnny. I should have a *say* in what happens to me, I've earned it with my own sweat. I've given nearly half my life to the Network.'

I said nothing. Pa said, 'And they're telling me it's redundancy. Johnny, there's no way that my job is redundant. What are they trying to say, that there's no need for a Network manager? That there's nowhere else they can fit me in? I'm a railway man through and through, John, I worked my way up from the bottom, there isn't a job in that organization that I can't do.'

'Take them to court, Pa,' I said proudly. 'Show them that they can't treat you like this.'

'It's these outsiders that Paddy Browne brought in. Corporate advisers, or whatever they are. Browne's trying to palm the responsibility off on to them. The Network's merely following their recommendations, he says. Here,' Pa said, handing over the letter of dismissal. 'But what I say, Johnny, is that these people have to work with the information they're given. And who was giving them the information? Browne. Browne was. Whereas me, I didn't even get to meet these people. I don't even know who they are. I wasn't consulted,' Pa said again. 'I wasn't consulted once.'

I looked at the letter. Pressing business needs, it said, necessitated a radical restructuring of the Network. An independent external report recommended severe cost-cutting. Unfortunately, this unavoidably entailed a degree of decruitment . . .

Pa gave me another piece of paper. It was headed, in his writing, PLAN OF ACTION. 'You see, I've got a battle plan. I'm not going to rush into anything without first having thought it through. If you're going to take on an outfit like the Network, you've got to have a strategy. It's no good just charging in head-first; you've got to do it step by step.' He rolled his sleeves down and began to button them at the wrist. 'They're going to find out, with a nasty shock, exactly who it is they're dealing with here.' He said, 'If they think that I'm just some pushover who'll gratefully pocket his severance money and go away, they're sorely mistaken.'

I studied the plan.

GOALS? REINSTATEMENT. STRATEGY? UNFAIR DISMISSAL PROCEEDINGS / NEGOTIATED SETTLEMENT THEREOF. COST-EFFICIENCY? GOOD. TIME-EFFICIENCY? ADEQUATE. DOWN-SIDE? TIME, MODERATE EXPENDITURE. ALTERNATIVE? COMPENSATION. TIMETABLE? 1. SEE LAWYER. 2. ISSUE PROCEEDINGS. 3. CO-ORDINATE WITH UNION ACTION. 4. ENCOURAGE OTHERS TO SUE.

So this was Pa's quick response to the problem. Mark Q. Fincham would have been proud of him.

I saw him waiting for a reaction. 'This is great,' I said. 'But do you really want to be reinstated? Don't you just want to take the money and run?'

'No,' Pa said emphatically. 'I'm not interested in the money; I'm interested in my job.'

Hiding my doubt, I said nothing to this.

'You wait and see,' he said. 'I'm going to make them take me back.'

I changed the subject. 'No sign of the dog, I suppose?' I said.

'Nope,' Pa said, checking the sliding door he had fixed. 'But she'll be back. She knows her way home. You can drop a dog a hundred miles away and still it'll make it back.' He pushed at the sliding door and bent at the knees. 'Don't you worry about Trusty, she'll be fine.' He caught my eye and slowly straightened, groaning cheerfully. 'I tell you what. If you're concerned about it, why don't the two of us go down to the dogs' home tomorrow, to see if she's turned up there? OK? Meet me here at ten.'

'OK,' I said.

'You're looking a bit down in the mouth,' Pa said. 'Is everything all right?'

'Everything's fine,' I said. 'I'm just a little . . .' I shrugged.

'What's the matter? Is it Rosie? Is something wrong at home?'

I shook my head. 'Nothing's wrong. Everything's fine.'

'Are you sure? Johnny?'

'Sure I'm sure,' I said, laughing. 'I'm just tired, that's all.'

'Just as long as you're not worrying about me,' Pa said, as he resumed his work on the door. 'You just think about yourself.

At your stage of life you've got to look out for number one. Concentrate on your chairs. You finished them yet?' I nodded without enthusiasm. 'That's great,' my father said. 'Did you know that I've got about twenty of the guys coming to the exhibition? Now that half of them have been laid off, they won't have any excuse not to come. And with their golden handshakes, they may even be able to buy something. No cloud without a silver lining, eh, Johnny?'

I could just see it: twenty awkward, brown-suited ex-middle-managers turning up at Devonshire's with my father at their head, all searching for a nonexistent exhibition. 'I've got to go,' I said. 'I'll see you tomorrow.'

'Why don't you come around tonight for a bite to eat?' Pa said. 'Bring Rosie, too. She can bring Steve if she wants. I'll cook some steaks.'

'I don't think I can, Pa,' I said untruthfully. 'I'm seeing Angela.'

'Well, tell her to come, too. She's always welcome, you know that. Besides, I haven't seen her for ages. How is she?'

I said, Good. Pa said, 'I'll leave it up to you. If you two want to come by, come by. If not, that's fine too.'

I did not go straight back to the flat. It was a hot day and I had nothing to do, so I decided instead to stroll around the neighbourhood in case there was any sign of Trusty. I did not share Pa's faith in her homing instinct. I knew that dog. She didn't know her ass from her elbow.

So I walked around the blocks that embodied the Rockportian dream of order, an undilapidated world of immaculate gardens, freshly painted frontages, upkeep and more upkeep, and kept a look-out. It was clear, from posters newly displayed on the windows of houses, that I was not the only one being vigilant. The posters, depicting a large eye peeled open against an orange backdrop, were the sign of the neighbourhood watch scheme and, judging by the number of eyes that stared unblinkingly down on the street, the whole community was on red alert, as though wild beasts and not harmless pets roamed abroad and these flawless, peaceful streets were sinister as jungles.

There was no sign of Trusty anywhere, of those black and

brown ears dangling in front of the sturdy, stumpy little body with the raised white-tipped tail, whippy as a car aerial, the sad, red-rimmed, sagging eyes, the neatly tailored rows of nipples. I tried the gardens, I tried the streets, I tried the field where she had been jumped on that first time by that police dog and where I had played my first games of football. There were still youngsters out on that grass today, still using jerseys as goalposts and still arguing furiously, as I had at their age, about the height of the nonexistent crossbar which connected the nonexistent uprights.

14

For no apparent reason, the train has stopped in some cutting in the middle of nowhere. All that is visible is a steep, grassy upslope topped by the blue slat of the sky.

The old lady says, 'We're not there already, are we?'

'No, madam, we're not,' the man says. 'The non-stop express,' he says, 'has stopped.' He stands up, opens the window and fruitlessly cranes his head outside. 'The very least they could do is tell us what the problem is. But of course they don't. They just leave us here to rot in ignorance in their stinking carriages. I mean, just look at the state of this seat, look at all this dirt. When was the last time they washed these things?'

The carriage door opens. It's the conductor.

My fellow traveller does not miss his chance. 'Excuse me,' he says loudly, 'what's the reason for this delay? How long are we going to be sitting here for?'

The conductor shrugs. 'I don't know,' he says. 'We've got a red light, that's all I can tell you. It could be anything.' He takes my ticket, a weekend return to Waterville, and stamps it.

'Well, why don't you find out? Or is that asking too much?'

The conductor looks the man in the eye. 'Listen, pal, I've told you what I know, all right? There's going to be an announcement soon, OK?' He turns and walks away.

I get up before the man can speak to me again and leave for the smoking compartment. I light a cigarette, blowing the smoke through a window.

When I got back to the trashed flat from Pa's on Monday afternoon, the answering machine was waiting for me with five red winks, one wink for every message. The first message was from Steve. 'Uh, hello, it's me. I'm down at the police station. I'll be here for a bit yet. I . . .' Steve stopped talking evidently because he was being spoken to. 'OK,' I heard him say. Then he said, 'Hello? I – ' and was cut off. He had run out of coins. Typical. He couldn't even make a telephone call without screwing up.

Then I thought, Police station? Steve had been *arrested*?

I became aware that Simon Devonshire's voice was speaking. 'John, I'm ringing about the chairs, which I received this afternoon. I think we've got a problem. Could you get back to me straight away?' The next message was his, too, as was the next. 'John, get back to me on this, urgently,' Devonshire repeated abruptly. 'I mean it.'

The last message was from Angela. 'John, this is me. Sorry about last night, I couldn't . . . I'll explain later.' She paused, allowing in background noise; she was ringing from a callbox. 'We need to talk.' Again there was a commotion. 'I'll ring you. Bye.'

For a second I felt a strong relief: she was fine, thank God. Then there was anxiety. Why had she sounded so shifty? Since when did we need to talk?

I called her at work. This time I got through.

'Where the hell have you been?'

'I've been working, Johnny. It's been awful.'

'Well, why didn't you call me? I waited for you all of last night.'

'I couldn't,' Angela said. 'I was in a meeting the whole time. I'm sorry, Johnny.'

I said flatly, 'I don't understand it, Angela. I don't understand why you couldn't make one simple call. It just doesn't make sense.' I waited for her to respond. She didn't. I said, 'What the hell is this job, anyway, that you're working on it for the whole of a Sunday night?'

She was silent. She began to say something then stopped.

I felt a pang of nausea. She was hiding something from me. I loved her and she was lying to me.

I said, 'What did you mean when you said in your message that we needed to talk?'

She hesitated. 'Well, we haven't been seeing much of each other recently and I thought that, well, you know, we should meet.'

'Well, I've been ready to meet for the last month. You've just never been around.'

Angela sighed. 'I know, I know, it's my fault.'

There was a pause. I said, 'Look, never mind. Why don't I meet you at your place tonight? I'll cook some pasta and maybe you could get a bottle of wine. We'll have an evening in, just the two of us.'

'Darling, I can't make it tonight. I'm going to some thing with clients. And then from tomorrow I'm away for three days.'

I was too hurt to say anything.

Angela said, 'My darling, I'm so sorry. I was thinking that we might see each other on Monday.'

'What, next week? That's seven days away, for Christ's sake. Are you saying that you can't fit me in in the next seven days? Is that what you're saying? Angela, what the hell is going on? Are you seeing somebody? Is that it?'

'Don't be like that, Johnny,' she said. 'Look, I've got an idea: why don't we meet tomorrow lunchtime. I've got half an hour. We'll have a sandwich at the gym. OK? Meet me there at one o'clock. OK? Johnny?'

'Yes,' I said, and I hung up abruptly. I waited for her to call back, but she didn't.

Devonshire did, though, and as soon as I heard his voice I hung up.

I picked up my cigarettes and went out. I didn't want to be around when he rang back again.

I decided to go to the police station, which was only a five-minute walk from the flat, to see what kind of a mess Steve had got himself into now. A worrying thought had occurred to me. Maybe it was Steve, finally pushed over the edge, who had smashed up the flat. Maybe Steve had hurt Rosie.

I spoke to the officer at the reception desk. 'I'm looking for Stephen Manus,' I said. 'The name is Breeze. I live with him. He rang me from here.'

The policeman looked at his paper and scratched his goatee thoughtfully. 'I'll check,' he said finally.

I waited standing up. Moments later a door opened and a group of bedraggled men emerged. They were, I saw, Rockport United supporters, almost certainly the ones who had rioted after the game. Judging by their sheepish demeanour, red eyes and dirty T-shirts, these men had spent a night and a day in the cells and their indocility was well and truly exhausted. I moved aside from the reception window as they obediently scribbled forms, their signatures ornate and unintelligible, like the signatures of children.

The receptionist returned. 'We've tracked Mr. Manus down, sir,' he said. 'He's helping us with our enquiries at the moment. You'll have to wait a few minutes until his interview is over.' He looked at the United fans, who had remained uncertainly in the lobby. 'All right, lads, you can go home now.' They trailed out. 'What a bunch of losers,' he said.

I sat down on a hard bench and lit a cigarette. Helping the police with their enquiries. Shit. Everybody knew what that meant.

'Johnny.'

I looked up. From a door to my left, Steve had come in. A brown stitched-up gash ran diagonally from his eyebrow to his hairline.

'Jesus, Steve, what's happened? Are you all right?'

He took a cigarette from me. 'I'm fine.'

'Why are you here? What have you done?'

'I haven't done anything. I'm a witness,' he said, pronouncing the word with solemn emphasis. Seeing my confusion, he began to speak quickly, grinning in his excitement. 'I went out on Sunday evening to get some milk, right? So, anyway, I'm coming back and about twenty yards from home I see this bloke running out of one of the houses on the street, number 6 I think it was, and he's carrying a hi-fi or something. I don't know why, but I can tell immediately that he's a burglar, so I approach him and, well, I jump on him just as he tries to get into his car.' Steve tapped his cigarette. 'I thought, you know, that I might, you know – make a citizen's arrest.'

'A citizen's arrest?'

'That's right,' Steve said. 'Anyway, he hit me and I fell and knocked my head.' Steve pointed at his head. 'Then he legs it down the road and then, I don't know why, I run after him.'

'You *ran*?' I couldn't imagine it.

'Yes,' Steve said. 'So, I catch up with the guy – don't forget, he's carrying his gear – and then' – here he hooped his arms –

'then I sort of tackle him.' He took a drag of his cigarette. 'So the two of us go down, and this bloke lands face-first on the hi-fi he's carrying, and suddenly it's like he's really bleeding and lying there moaning. Meanwhile, I'm bleeding as well, and so there's blood everywhere. Then before we can move, this police car arrives and picks him up.'

I shook my head. 'Steve, what can I say? That's amazing. To be honest, well, I never thought that . . .' I abandoned the remark. 'Fantastic,' I said. 'Well done. So, last night you were . . .'

'In hospital. Because of this,' he said, pointing at his scar. 'Sixteen stitches. I should have rung, I know, but . . .' He made an apologetic movement. 'I suppose Rosie must have been worried?'

'You could say that,' I said, thinking of the flat.

At this point, a woman in a track suit who had been loitering within earshot for some time approached Steve and said, 'I'm sorry, but I couldn't help overhearing what you were saying. I'm from the *Rockport Crier*. Would you mind if I asked you some questions?'

'Well,' Steve said, smiling coyly, 'I'm not sure you'll find it very interesting.'

The woman laughed. 'Don't worry, we'll make it interesting,' she said. She extracted a portable telephone from her handbag. 'Do you mind if I call our photographer?'

Steve raised his eyebrows in excitement. 'Wow,' he said, 'no.'

The reporter brought out a pocket tape-recorder and the man in my sister's life told his story again. Shortly afterwards, the photographer arrived, and after a short conversation with the reporter it was decided to wrap a bandage around Steve's head for dramatic effect. Steve did not mind. They lined him up outside the police station and photographed him standing there like a war hero.

That is how, the next day, a photograph of a smiling Steve, a tussock of hair sprouting above the head bandage, appeared in the *Crier*. There was an accompanying caption.

MAN OF THE MONTH. *Have-a-go hero Steve Manus, 29, who on Sunday single-handedly grabbed a dangerous burglar in north*

Redrock. 'It was nothing,' Steve said last night from hospital. 'Anyone else would have done the same.' The Crier disagrees. Jobless Steve showed the kind of gallantry this city badly needs. That's why we're making him our Man of the Month. Well done, Steve!

The headline read, TO CATCH A THIEF.

The train groans and moves forward a few feet before stopping again. I throw my cigarette stub out of the window.

Headlines.

Here's another one for the scrapbook: FREAK LIGHTNING KILLS WOMAN, 34.

She was wearing a pink track suit. She was running across the town square on the way to the gym. There was not so much as a drop falling from the sky.

I light up another cigarette. The train still isn't going anywhere.

I read the piece about Steve on Tuesday morning, on my way to meeting Pa to accompany him to the municipal kennels. When I rang the doorbell of the house there was no response at all. I went around the house into the back garden and saw that, up on the first floor, the curtains of his bedroom were still drawn. He was in, it seemed, but for some reason he was not answering. I went in through the back door, using the key he hides under the third flowerpot in the shed.

I found him in the near-darkness of his room, lying as usual on his side of the bed, my mother's vacant half still topped off by two separate unwrinkled pillows. Although his eyes were closed, I could tell he wasn't sleeping.

I sat down on the edge of the bed. 'Pa,' I said softly. 'Pa. The kennels. We're supposed to be going to the kennels. To look for Trusty.' There was no response. He remained completely motionless, his eyes bunched shut into purple knots, like blackberries.

Eventually, I said, 'I'm going to go down and make us tea, OK? Pa? Then we're going to go. OK?'

He didn't answer.

I went down and made two cups of tea and a couple of slices of toast just the way he liked them, with thick-cut marmalade.

'OK, come and get it,' I shouted up. 'Breakfast.' But he did not come and get it; there was no heavy, flat-footed descent of the stairs and no subsequent slurping of tea, no annoying clinking of the spoon in the cup.

I went up with the breakfast on a tray.

'Have some of this,' I said. I touched him lightly on the shoulder. 'Come on.' I started to drink my own tea to encourage him. 'Have some toast, it's getting cold.'

But again, he just lay there. On the wall over his bed were the yellow Post-it stickers upon which he had scribbled down the brainwaves which had occurred to him in the nights, rough jottings which in the light of day never did justice to the flickering and boundless notions they sought to capture. All the same, my father has persisted with them, these mistranslations of his dreams, hopeful that one morning he will awake and simply peel from the wall the solution to his conundrums.

'Pa?' No answer.

So this was it, his first day of unemployment. The fighting spirit he had shown the day before was revealed for what it was, the short-lived euphoria which a misfortune of special purity can occasion. It had finally happened: the punishment had taken its toll and at last he was out for the count. I looked at him, a shapeless bulge under the bedclothes. When, watching Muhammad Ali fighting Joe Frazier as a kid, I had said to him, 'Pa, you could beat them, couldn't you? Couldn't you, Pa?' he had replied without hesitation, 'Of course I could. Your old dad could lick those guys, no problem.'

'Look, you just take it easy,' I said to him. 'I'll go to the kennels on my own.' I fished the car keys out of his jacket. 'I'll be back later. All right?' There was no reply, and so I got up to leave.

When I reached the door, I heard him mumble something. 'What was that?' I said.

'Merv's dead,' he said.

'Pa,' I said, 'I – '

'Go away, John. Leave me alone now.'

The train starts up its whining, rumbling engine.

Merv Rasmussen. I can see him on the tennis court, serving underarm because his hump, big as a boulder under the sweaty, clinging white shirt, does not permit a full overhead swing of the racquet . . . Despite the handicap, Merv was a more talented, less erroneous player than my father, the one with the groundstrokes and the positional sense to play the odd winner. But the two of them – at least, on the two or three times when, for one reason or another, I watched them play their doubles matches, usually from the vacant umpire's seat – never blamed or criticized one another. In fact, they said very little to each other at all, even after the game, when they sat in their track suits and drank a shandy each at the club bar. They simply enjoyed being there together – or, more accurately perhaps, not being there; because when they played they must surely have embraced the self-vanishing possibilities of the sport, so that for the duration of a set or two and of a drink thereafter there would be a welcome respite, a time-out, from the existences of Eugene Breeze and Mervyn Rasmussen, railway executives, family men, taxpayers and whatever other onerous identities they laboured under off the court.

Well, Merv has certainly been released from himself now; only Merv is not playing tennis.

15

The train has started moving again, rumbling uncomfortably as it slowly eases free of the embankment and open fields, efficiently sprinkled with cows, come into view. I return to my seat.

The lady is worrying out loud about her dog. 'My nephew,' she is saying, 'he's a doctor, he usually takes the dog in while I'm away, but he can't today because he's away at a conference. He'd said he'd be back on the Friday, but now he won't be able to come back until the Sunday. Or until this evening, at the earliest. Not before Saturday night, that's what he said.' She rubs at a bump on her face. 'I'm just hoping that nothing has happened to her. She's all alone in the house and she won't understand it. The girl next door is supposed to feed her, but she's very particular about who feeds her and I'm just worried that she won't eat. She's a very nervous dog, the vet said so. He said she needs a lot of affection, and she gets terribly upset if I'm away.'

The man makes a noise of acknowledgement but continues to read his paper.

Dogs. When I arrived at the dogs' home on Tuesday morning I asked the fellow at the enquiries desk – Tony, his badge said – whether a basset bitch had made an appearance. 'She should be wearing a blue collar and a disc with her name on it – Trusty Breeze.'

Shaking his head gloomily, Tony, a thin man with a scrupulously ironed white T-shirt, tapped into his computer. 'I don't think so. We've got a basset, as it happens, but I don't think she's called Trusty.' He tapped again. 'Mabel,' he said. 'We've got a Mabel. That's a pretty name, isn't it?' He stood up and clasped his hands. 'Still, we'd better check, hadn't we?'

I followed him into a small covered courtyard surrounded by three levels of kennels on each side. It stank. The air resounded with yelps, barks and howls of every kind. Apart from the greyhounds – and there were greyhounds everywhere, silently curled up into sad balls – I couldn't identify the breed of any of these strays, their snouts looming from the dark cells as they pressed against the grilles. They were all mongrels, it seemed, unbred, unwanted nothing dogs.

Tony stopped. 'This is she,' he said.

Inside the cell, the sleeping dog lifted its head a fraction from its front paws and opened a baggy red eye. It paused for a slothful moment, regarding us. Then it slowly got up, shook itself, and came forward hopefully, tail waving.

The cage was too dark for me to be sure. I went down on my haunches to get a better look. 'Trusty,' I said. 'Trusty.' No response. 'Mabel,' I said, and immediately the dog reacted, barking.

I stood up, defeated.

Everywhere locked-up dogs bayed in frustration or lay slumped and dispirited. 'What happens to them all?' I asked.

'Well, we keep them for a week, and then we assess them, and then the suitable ones are put forward for the sales,' Tony said. 'Most of them find new homes, you know.'

'What about the ones that don't?'

'Well, we have to think of the dog's welfare,' Tony said defensively. 'If it can't be found a home, or if it's sick, well, we have to put it to sleep.'

We looked at Mabel. She was gaping at us expectantly, her mouth slightly ajar. 'They'll be plenty of takers for her, I'll bet,' I said, trying to find something positive to say.

He looked pained. 'Well, actually, no,' he said. 'Mabel is unsuitable for sale. She's very aggressive, poor thing. She bites everything that moves. I was hoping that you might be her owner.'

I left the dogs' home depressed. Trusty had been missing now for two nights and a day.

But, I thought to myself as I drove back to Pa's, you couldn't blame her for running away. She had been rampantly on heat, after all, and when the burglars had broken in she had quite naturally grabbed the opportunity to break out. Trusty had responded to a call of the wild which was not of her making.

Good luck to her. Let her have her shot at true freedom, at

finding an alternative to the human regimen. Even dogs must long for escape, for some alternative.

The problem was, there was no alternative to living at home with Pa. Rockport was not a hospitable wilderness in which she might thrive, with grassland where a pack of fellow hunters could be found and joined; there was only the city and its streets, and that was no environment for a dog, certainly not one as domesticated as Trusty. Trusty's normal routine was a bowl of cornflakes and a slice of strawberry jam toast in the morning, followed by a quick turn around the block with Pa before he set off for the office, followed by a day spent snoozing around the house, followed by another, longer, walk and some lamb chops or spaghetti carbonara or whatever else Pa was cooking up in the evening, and then maybe a late-night stroll in the moonlight. Trusty was not accustomed to rifling through rubbish pails at dawn or drinking from puddles. I pictured her stumpily wandering around Rockport, frightened and disoriented. All it would take would be one speeding car and, bang, that would be it, curtains. No one had ever said that dogs enjoyed an afterlife.

But what more could I do? Offer a reward? Put up HAVE YOU SEEN THIS DOG? posters? It was bad enough having pictures of my father plastered all over the place.

I opened the front door of the house, dropped the car keys on the entranceway table and walked through. There was no sign of my father. Don't tell me he was still in bed.

Up I went. Yes, there he was, just as I had left him two hours ago, curled beneath his duvet as disconsolately as one of those abandoned greyhounds. The cup of tea I had placed next to his bed had not been touched.

I did not try to stir him. I simply said, 'Trusty's not at the kennels. If any basset hound turns up, they'll let us know.' He did not respond. I stood there for a moment. 'Here,' I said, putting that morning's issue of the *Crier* next to his bed. 'When you get up, you may want to take a look at page three. You'll be in for a nice surprise.'

He rolled over on to his other shoulder, turning his back to me.

I took a seat on a chair cushioned with dirty clothes and

began to smoke a cigarette. I became more insistent. 'Look,' I said, 'you can't just lie here all day. It's twelve-thirty. Please, Pa, get up. Please.' More silence. I gave up. I had to go. I was meeting Angela at one. 'I'll be back tonight,' I said. 'OK?'

I went to the bathroom, rinsed my mouth with toothpaste and checked myself in the mirror: clean-shaven, wearing the black crew-neck which she had bought me as a birthday present, and jeans. Not too bad – but then not too great either, with the slightly overlong nose and colourless skin of the Breezes.

I caught the bus to the city centre.

It took me a couple of attempts to find the discreet entry to Angela's gym, which was hidden in the basement of an office block occupied by an insurance company. I went down the stairs and stood uncertainly in the lobby, a light-filled, cream-carpeted space where tropical trees sprang vigorously from barrels of earth and green murals depicted shoals of fish. Symbols on the wall pointed towards a restaurant/bar, a swimming pool, a sauna and rooms for aerobics, weights and changing clothes. I approached the receptionist, a young woman dressed like a banker, and stated the purpose of my visit. She responded by producing a bright yellow visitor's badge and pinning it to my chest. 'I suggest that you wait in the bar,' she said, turning towards another arrival.

I followed the signs, going past glass-walled exercise rooms where perspiring professionals ran, rowed and cycled while they gazed at televisions hanging from the ceiling. I had just caught sight of the restaurant entrance when to my left I noticed a young woman with red boxing gloves attacking the pads held up by a fitness instructor. It was Angela, her long neck glistening beneath the dark rope of her hair.

She was wearing dark blue Adidas cycling shorts and a white T-shirt which adhered to her damp compacted breasts, the nipples plainly visible. The instructor, his body a pure aggregate of muscle, loomed enormously over her. Give me three, I could hear him say, now give me three more, and she reacted automatically to his commands, hitting the pads with a grimace of determination. Jab, jab, jab, the instructor shouted, and again she obeyed, her slender arms shuddering as they uncoiled towards him.

On she went, oblivious of my presence on the other side of the glass, now launching a combination of uppercuts, now holding up her hands and simply moving her feet. Keep moving, shouted the trainer, keep that head down. Angela threw more punches, a series of hooks this time, and then more still. She began to grunt with the effort, grunting every time she threw a punch: uh, *thud*, uh, *thud*, uh, *thud*.

I felt myself physically weakening. I had no idea that she boxed.

OK, that's three minutes, the instructor said, unlacing her gloves. Let's warm down.

He pulled out a mat and they lay down on their backs alongside each other, their legs slowly flexing in unison. Then he got up, and while Angela stayed on her back and continued with leg exercises, he began firmly massaging her temples and her scalp, her head disappearing into his huge hands.

I couldn't watch any longer. I went to the bar and bought myself a bottle of beer.

She came in five minutes later fully dressed, washed hair pulled tightly back from her face, cheeks flushed. She looked beautiful and strange. 'Darling,' she said, and she kissed me, and I smelled the smell she has.

We sat down at a table next to the windows that gave on to an interior courtyard with a pool and ferns. 'I'm starving,' Angela said. 'Let's order straight away.'

I looked at the menu: expensive. A tenner for a grilled chicken sandwich. And that was the cheapest item.

Angela said, 'Don't worry, have what you want. This is on me.'

'Why? Have you had another pay rise?' I asked ironically.

She looked coyly at her menu.

I said, 'You haven't really, have you?'

'Well, yes, I have,' she admitted, smiling shyly.

'Well? What are you on?'

'Johnny, that's embarrassing.'

'Embarrassing? This is me you're talking to, remember.' I waited for a reply. 'So?'

She hesitated, then looked at me. Her eyes were still that deep, dark blue. 'Sixty,' she said.

Sixty thousand.

That was almost twice what Pa made – had made. That was almost ten times what I could hope to scratch together in a year.

I kept cool. 'They've doubled your salary,' I said. 'Nice one.' I reached for my cigarettes.

'You can't smoke here, Johnny. It's a health club. I'm sorry, I should have told you.'

'That's all right,' I said. I glanced around the room. I was the only man who didn't have freshly combed wet hair and who wasn't wearing a suit.

The food arrived. I ordered another bottle of beer.

We started eating. 'It's been a while since we've done this,' I said. 'I hardly know what to say.'

'I know, Johnny, I'm sorry.' Angela said, 'I've missed you, you know. You're looking very handsome.'

I said, 'I was so worried on Sunday night, I was so worried that something had happened.' I touched her leg with mine. 'Things haven't been easy,' I said. 'We've had some bad news. Pa's been fired.'

She looked at me, clearly upset. 'I know, it's terrible,' I said. I sighed. 'He's not taking it well, you know. It's knocked the stuffing out of him.'

'Johnny,' Angela said. 'Johnny, I . . .' She reached across the table and took my hands in hers.

A bleeping noise suddenly emanated from under the table. Angela reached down and retrieved a mobile telephone from her briefcase. She spoke briefly with the caller, then said, 'I have to go, my love.' She rose to her feet.

I said, 'But we haven't finished our food.'

I stood up and followed her to the till. Once outside in the sunshine, we kissed, and it was wonderful to feel her ribcage pressed against mine and her moist, giving mouth. I held her by the waist and said, 'We're all right, aren't we?' She blinked affirmatively. 'When are we seeing each other again? Does it have to be Monday? Can't it be sooner?'

'I'm supposed to be in Waterville for the rest of the week,' she said. 'But I'll try,' she said. 'I'll call you, darling.'

I walked her back to her office and watched her disappear

through the massive revolving door. I caught a bus home, feeling a little better about things. Then I thought, how come she never told me she had a mobile phone? Why don't I have the number?

I became aware of a needling pain behind my right eyeball.

The bus reached my stop. I alighted and walked heavily home. Peace and quiet. That was what I needed now. Rest.

Rosie was back. She was sitting in the squalor, smoking a cigarette. She had kicked off her shoes but, this detail apart, she was in full uniform – hat, scarf and all. Steve was in the kitchen.

I remained standing on the threshold of the sitting-room. I toed aside some pieces of smashed crockery. 'Well?' I said. 'What are you going to do about this?' I kicked at a paperback, sending it fluttering against the wall.

'I'll clear it up,' Rosie said flatly. She switched on the television and stared intently at the images of an afternoon game show.

'Well, just do it soon,' I said. I made sure, by the tone of my voice, that she understood that I was serious.

At this point, a choice of action presented itself. I could either go to my bedroom and slam the door behind me in my displeasure; or, having said my piece, I could be amicable and try to foster an atmosphere of goodwill, love and harmony – what is sometimes known as a family atmosphere. I had a headache. I chose concord.

'So, what's new?' I said.

Rosie changed channels with a jab of her thumb.

I restrained myself by walking through to the kitchen. 'How's our hero?' I said, switching on the kettle.

'OK,' Steve replied, mumbling. He pointed questioningly to his mouth, which was full of cheese and bread.

'That's OK,' I said, 'help yourself.' I opened the refrigerator. A segment of beef tomato, raspberry jam, margarine. No milk. I rose tiredly. Steve yes, milk no. In the chaos of the universe, certain things remained fixed.

I abandoned any thought of making myself a coffee and a sandwich and headed for my room. Just as I was about to exit, I turned and said to Rosie, who had not moved from her seat,

'So when are you going to start? Are you just going to sit there while the rest of us have to put up with this – ' I shouted the word – 'this *shit*?' I scooped up half of a plate with my foot and with a swing of the leg sent it flying against the wall, where it broke into still smaller pieces. 'Just who the fuck do you think you are?' I shouted.

Rosie stood up. 'How dare you? I clean this place up every time I come home. You and him just sit here all day doing *nothing*. I'm always clearing up after you, *always*.' Her voice grew high-pitched. '*You* should be clearing this up, it's about bloody time that *you* did something for me for a change.'

I was not going to take this. I picked up a hard green apple from the fruitbowl and hurled it as hard as I could two feet or so wide of her head at the far wall. With a splat, half of the apple disintegrated, leaving a wet patch and debris on the wallpaper. Steve took cover behind the opened door of the fridge. 'Do you think you can fuck up the whole flat and expect us to say nothing about it? You fucking terrorize us with your fucking moods, you smash up these plates given to the both of us by Pa, plates which I fucking *own*, and you don't give a shit! You just do it without a fucking thought for anyone else! Well, here,' I shouted, grabbing a framed photograph belonging to her which had remained on the bookcase, 'here, I don't give a shit either.' I stamped repeatedly on the photograph, pulverizing the glass and wrecking the snapshot of a sun-tanned Rosie on holiday in Spain.

'Stop it,' she said, 'stop it, Johnny.'

I kicked the photograph aside. I was close to tears myself. I said, 'Rosie, this is the kind of crap which you put us through the whole time. Look, just look at what you've done: you've completely wrecked the flat! I mean, are you crazy or what? Maybe you should see a doctor, I don't know. Do you think this is normal? What's the matter with you?' There was a quaver in my voice. Rosie was hunched forward on the edge of the sofa, sniffing and pointing her face at her toes. Had her hair been long it would have fallen before her face, but now that hiding-place was gone. 'You can't go on like this,' I continued, speaking more gently. 'You've got to start giving some thought to what other people are going through. You're not the only one with problems. Everybody's got problems. Look at Pa: did you know that he's been fired?' Rosie stiffened. 'That's right, Pa's been fired,' I said. 'At this moment he's lying in bed with the curtains drawn, and you don't even know about it.' My voice was hoarse. 'Oh, yes; and Merv Rasmussen has died.'

I went to my room and dropped face-down on the bed.

That was at four in the afternoon. When I awoke, still in my clothes, it was seven in the evening and the window was a faint pink rectangle. My headache had gone and the house was quiet. I moved slightly, turned the pillow over to its cool side and closed my eyes again.

The telephone began ringing. I tensed. I was not going to answer it because it had to be Devonshire. I could picture him at the other end of the line, the brutal contours of the blazer, the fury mounting each time a bleep of the call went unanswered by me, a pipsqueak whom he had done such a great favour.

Nobody picked up the phone. The ringing stopped as the answering machine was activated. I got out of bed and went to play the message. 'This is Whelan,' the voice said, 'of Whelan Lock & Key. I'm ringing to say that I can come round this Saturday, if you like. Thank you.'

A shriek of laughter came from Rosie's room. The door crashed open and my sister stumbled out, still laughing dementedly. A rolled-up sock flew at her from the bedroom, flung by her boyfriend in a parody of violence. Rosie was clutching a copy of the *Crier* and pointing convulsively at the photograph of Steve. Unbalanced in her merriment, she plunged on to the sofa and smothered her gleeful screams into the cushions. I started grinning, too, because Rosie's laughter is air scooped from the lungs and expelled in the purest, most infectious note of hilarity, and also because the sight of her animated is always in itself a relief and a joy.

'Look,' she said, her eyes wet, 'look.'

'I know,' I said. 'I thought you knew. It's wonderful, isn't it?'

She could barely speak. 'Man of the Month,' she whispered, shuddering with mirth, 'Man of the Month.'

Steve came in, tucking his shirt into his trousers and sheepishly smiling. Rosie pointed at him, uttered the words 'Man of the Month', and started shrieking all over again. Her haircut wasn't bad at all, I thought, once you got used to it.

'Get me the phone, my hero,' she said to Steve, who complied. Still chortling, Rosie ordered a pizza supreme and six beers for delivery. 'My warrior,' she said, handing him back the telephone. 'We're going to celebrate the fame which you have brought to this house. Now get me the duvet,' she ordered, 'and bring me the TV guide.' Steve obeyed, and the two of them settled down on the sofa face to face, their legs interlocked beneath the quilt.

The room, already oppressive in its disarray, shrank with their happiness. I put on my jacket. 'I'm going to Pa's,' I said. 'I'll leave you two lovebirds to get on with it.'

'I'll call him tomorrow,' Rosie said. 'I promise. I'm just not up to it now. I'll call him first thing.'

16

I arrived at the house to find that my father had finally got out of bed. He was sitting downstairs in the living-room in a vest and pyjama bottoms, a can of Heineken in his hand. The curtains were drawn and the room's darkness was relieved only by the luminosity of the television, a fifteen-year-old black-and-white portable which he had brought down from the spare room. He was watching football. I recognized the team in dark-and-light: Rockport United. It was a programme about last Sunday's game.

I fetched a beer, too, and took over an armchair on the other side of the room.

They were showing Ballybrew's fateful last-minute free kick. The picture froze just as the kick was about to be taken. The analyst, a distinguished former international, drew a white arrow from the ball to the corner of the goal. 'This is where Burke is aiming – to the goalkeeper's, Taylor's, left. That's at least thirty-five yards away. Now, unless you're Koeman or Cantona or one of the other great strikers of the ball, your chance of scoring from there is very remote indeed. I question the need for having a wall there at all.' The analyst paused for emphasis. 'Now take a look at what happens next.' Burke hoofed the ball in slow motion. 'The ball hits the wall, deviates to the keeper's right and ends up in the back of the net. There.' He circled the ball. 'So if Burke's kick had gone as intended, there would not have been a goal, because the keeper had his left corner covered and would have saved it. And if United had not been extra cautious and had not put a wall in front of the kicker, there wouldn't have been a goal either.' We were returned to the studio, where the three members of the panel were grinning ruefully. 'Sometimes you just can't win,' the analyst said, laughing.

'Rubbish,' Pa said forcibly. 'They're just rubbish. I'll never waste my time on that team again.' He looked at me. Threadbare silver stubble sprouted from his soft face like grass in poor soil. 'You want another beer?' I shook my head. Barefooted, he went to the kitchen to help himself. His toenails, hard, shining curves in the half-light, needed cutting.

The curtains were billowing. I went over to investigate.

'Pa, the windows are completely broken. Anybody could walk in.'

'What do you want me to do, call that clown Whelan? Anyway, what does it matter? If somebody wants to come in here, that's fine by me.' Pa fell into his chair with a fresh can. 'As far as I'm concerned, they can all come in and help themselves. I mean it.' He made a sweeping gesture. 'The TV, the chairs, the lot. It's all theirs.'

I didn't react.

Fresh figures appeared on the television: athletes, lining up on their blocks for a sprint. Down they went, into a crouch, waiting. The starting pistol cracked, then cracked once more. A false start.

Perhaps it was just the light of the television and the shadows it pooled in the sockets of his eyes, but my father's pale face looked ghostlier than ever.

'Have you eaten, Pa?'

'I'm not hungry.'

'I'll make you some soup, if you like. I think I've seen some onion soup somewhere.'

'Son, I'm *not hungry.*'

The sprinters crouched once more. Crack. This time it was for real. They ran as fast as they could for a hundred metres.

It was all too dismal. 'What about Steve, eh?' I said, pointing at the discarded copy of the *Crier* on the floor. 'Who would have thought it?'

Pa took a sip from his can and shrugged. 'It's all phoney, all that Man of the Month stuff. It's all done to sell newspapers.'

'I know,' I said, 'but still . . .' Jesus, I had never known him to be so negative. 'I just think that it's great for Steve, that's all. I don't know, maybe this is the break he's been looking for.'

'Getting your picture in the papers doesn't mean a damn thing. Look at me, I've got my photograph all over Rockport.'

I said, with an actual flicker of conviction, 'Maybe this will be the turning-point for him; maybe this will give him the push he needs.'

Pa gave a dry laugh. 'John, let's not kid ourselves any longer about Steve: the boy's a complete washout.'

Hold on, I felt like saying, I've never deluded myself about Steve; you're the one who keeps saying what a great guy he is underneath it all.

'I think you're being harsh,' I said. 'It's not a small thing, what he did.'

'The fellow's a halfwit,' Pa said. 'Otherwise what would he be doing with Rosie?'

I could not believe what I had heard.

'Don't look so shocked, Johnny,' he said, pronouncing my name with a touch of mockery. 'Would *you* want her as your girlfriend? All that screaming and shouting and selfishness?' He tilted the last drops of Heineken down his throat. 'I've been doing some thinking,' he said. 'I've been sorting things out in my mind and seeing things as they are. See things as they really are,' he said. 'And I'm telling you, Rosie's no good.' He began to extend the fingers of his left hand one by one, numbering. 'She's selfish. She's mean-minded. She's unloving. She doesn't give a moment's thought either to me, or to you, or to Steve, or to anybody else.' He flicked his hand dismissively. 'Those are the facts.'

'She's your daughter.'

'So? She's nearly thirty. She can't ask us to suspend our judgements for ever. She takes and she takes and she takes. She never gives. Do remember what she said when I asked her to come and visit Merv? Do you remember?' Pa made a noise of disgust. 'She exploits everybody around her. She manipulates us all with her unhappiness.'

'She doesn't mean to be unkind,' I said. 'You think that she wouldn't change if she could?'

He stared at the television. 'I don't know,' he eventually said tiredly. 'I don't know anything any more.' He kept staring. A long-distance race was now in progress, the athletes bobbing along on the inside track.

I noticed a card on the floor. It was an invitation to the

cremation of Mr Mervyn Rasmussen, taking place the next day.

'Are you going to this?' I said. There was a silence. 'I'll come with you, if you like,' I said.

Pa asserted suddenly, 'You spend years, your whole life, making a family, a home, working, and then . . .' He clicked his fingers, making a small sound. 'What's the use.'

He was beginning to sound like me.

I said, 'You're bound to feel low. You've gone through a terrible patch which nobody deserves. The job, Merv Rasmussen, Jesus, even Trusty . . .'

'I don't care about the dog. I could get another dog tomorrow. They're all the same. They're just dogs.' He rubbed his eyes. 'Anyway, I'm better off without her. All she's ever been good for is . . .' He motioned tiredly at the carpet.

Around the track the runners went and then around once more. A small group broke free at the front.

Hoarsely, Pa said, 'I prayed for him, Johnny. I lit a candle for him.' He swallowed hard.

I felt angry on his behalf. 'I know,' I said. 'You did everything you could.'

'It's not right. It shouldn't happen.' He hesitated, his face a grimace. 'Where is God in all of this. Where does He fit in, Johnny?'

I knew the answer to that one, but I was not going to tell my father. Although, for the sake of his own well-being, I had wanted him to be more realistic about things, I didn't want him to be too realistic. I did not want him finishing up a no-hoper like me, good for nothing but inaction in the daytime and the shakes at night.

I stayed the night at Pa's, in my old bedroom. The window, set in a dormer in the rear roof of the house, gave upon the same old silhouettes of the dunes, and the bookshelf was as ever piled with the ancient, battered hardbacks of the adventures of Tintin. I threw my clothes on the floor, climbed into my childhood bed and worked through the books one after the other, summoned utterly to the familiar, funny, inextinguishable otherworld of *Red Rackham's Treasure*, *The Broken Ear* and *The Crab with the Golden Claws*. Time and again Tintin found himself in a tight spot from which, time and again, by hook or by crook, he slipped. Take *Tintin in America*. Every page ended with the boy reporter and his dog, Snowy, in a jam of one terrible kind or another: falling over a precipice, trussed up for a lynching, bound to a rail track with a train approaching, tossed into Lake Michigan with a dumb-bell tied to his feet – these were the hottest waters imaginable and yet somehow, wonderfully, Tintin always escaped.

Lights off. It was so quiet I could hear the sea arriving and rearriving on the strand half a mile away.

This was the room where I had first started making chairs. Even now there remained some wood shavings ingrained at the edges of the carpet, beyond the suck of the vacuum cleaner. What a crazy idea that was, that I might build a life around such an activity. I turned, and the murmur of sheets in my ear momentarily replaced the murmuring of the waves. Maybe things would be different if I had a decent job, one like Angela's, a job which impacted on people's lives . . .

The brooding, the doom and gloom, had to come to an end. And not just for my own peace of mind. Angela didn't like it. It made no sense to her that someone could be derailed by the simple knowledge of futility. Nobody else seemed to suffer from this problem, certainly no one at Bear Elias. Either that, or they hid it very well. Maybe that was the truth, that people toughed it out secretly, ashamed and anxious, without heroism. They kept busy, stopping up those loopholes in the day when one had nothing better to do than to fall into contemplation, those minutes which, in my case, invariably added up to the small, unlit hours. If you bent your back all day at the office and immediately followed that up with an evening with a hungry, exhausting family and then got up early the next morning and clocked in all over again, day in, day out, that, with luck, should do the trick: send you flying to dreamland the moment your head hit the pillow – like Angela.

A cold feeling of powerlessness overcame me.

I rolled on to my stomach, facing the wall. At least Pa was in bed now, with a glass of milk and half an orange inside him. I had peeled it for him myself and presented it to him on a saucer. What a marvellous package of nutrition, with its brightly dimpled, waterproof overcoat and its perfectly segmented contents. How could such a thing come to be?

I felt hopeful and sleepy. I remembered a green jungle bug which miraculously resembled, down to the last quirk, the leaves of the rare bush that was its habitat: what was the explanation for that wonderful creature? Holed up in this warm mystery, I fell asleep.

The next morning I arose purposefully and went down to the shops and bought newspapers and coffee and croissants. This, I determined as I returned in the new summery heat, was going to be a good day; a fresh start, even.

I entered the back way, through the kitchen. I shut the door and jumped, almost dropping my purchases. A shrill, unrelenting tintinnabulation had begun to sound wildly throughout the house. This was Pa's doing: he had fixed the burglar alarm so that it did not work.

I ran up the stairs in the din. He was still in bed, lying on his side with his head barely emerging from under the bedclothes. 'How do I switch off this racket?' I shouted. 'Pa!' I pushed at his unbudging shoulder. 'What's the matter with you? Get up. The bloody alarm's gone off! Can't you hear? Get up!' I shouted. I could feel his body tense at the touch of my hand. 'Pa!'

Pa turned and swung his arm like a backhand topspin smash and struck me on the right side of the face.

We stared at each other speechlessly. The alarm kept belling away.

Finally, he said, 'The cellar.' He pointed in no particular direction. 'The cellar. The red box.'

'What about it?'

'You pull it,' he said. 'The lever. You pull it.'

I switched off the alarm and stayed downstairs. I couldn't believe it. I couldn't believe what he'd done.

A few moments later the stairs groaned with his heavy tread. He came in, hands sheepishly buried in his dressing-gown pockets, and stood at the doorway for a few moments. He said, 'Johnny, I'm sorry. I just – '

I interrupted him. 'Forget it.'

He shook his head in dismay. 'I can't understand it. I . . . There's no excuse – '

'Pa, *forget* it,' I said. I inhaled from my cigarette. 'Now, do you want to go to this cremation or not? If you do, you'd better get dressed and get shaved. We've got to go in five minutes.'

'I don't think I'll be going.'

I said, 'Do what you want. He was your friend. If you don't want to go, that's fine with me.'

An expression of exhaustion crossed his face as he took a deep breath. He ran his fingers through his hair. 'OK. I'll be down in a minute.'

I switched on the television and watched a game show. Shortly afterwards Pa came down, wearing a black suit.

I drove the car, he gave monosyllabic directions. He knew the way. We were going to the place where the incineration of my mother's body, already half charred by the thunderbolt, had been completed.

Outskirts of Rockport passed by, the deep pavements plotted with intensely coloured grass. We arrived. I said, 'You go on in, Pa. I'll wait for you here.'

He sat there for a few moments, looking up at the red-bricked building at the top of the knoll. He had not shaved carefully and a tufty, dirty-white fringe of stubble showed under his nostrils. It was a lovely, slightly windy day. Daisies speckled the lawns of the crematorium.

'You'd better get going,' I said softly. I undid the catch of his seat belt. Slowly, he got out. I watched him trudge up the shallow slope, head down, body leaning forward.

I remained seated, smoking. One or two cars drove by. Then I looked up and saw that the doors of the building were closed. The proceedings were under way.

I knew the drill. The priest. The quiz-show organ music. The sudden alarm as the conveyor belt jolted into action. The irrevocable exit of my mother in her coffin through wine-red curtains into the wall. Then the small reception in the hospitality room, where strongly scented adults shook me and Rosie by the hand and kissed us. Unable to bear it, we made for the garden. That was a hot day, too, with bees at work everywhere, and I was happy enough sitting there on a bench in the sunshine until my sister touched my arm and pointed upwards at the black smoke escaping urgently from the tall cement chimney.

It was incomprehensible. I said, 'Do you really think that that's Ma? It's not, is it?'

'Of course it is,' Rosie said. 'She's being burned, isn't she?' She wrinkled her face. 'God, sometimes you're so *thick*.'

We went back inside. The reception was coming to an end and our father was speaking with the funeral director. 'Not for another hour or two,' the funeral director was saying. He was a cheerful, happy-looking man.

'We'll wait,' Pa said. 'I don't mind waiting.'

'There won't be any need for that,' the funeral director said. 'We'll look after everything. We'll telephone you when we're ready.' He looked at us with a kindly eye. 'The children will want to be going,' he said.

Pa was not listening. 'We'll wait,' he said. 'It's no bother.'

The funeral director said, 'Well, it's most unusual . . . And there'll be another cremation following shortly . . .'

'I'll be back in one hour,' my father said, taking Rosie and me by the hand.

We went to a coffee bar. From time to time, Pa started to say things. Rosie and I poured sugar in our Cokes to make them fizz. We weren't thirsty, anyway.

We went back to the crematorium. Pa said, 'Stay in the car, you two,' but we followed him anyway.

Pa said, 'I've come for my wife. Mary Breeze.'

The receptionist said, 'If you would take a seat for a moment.' Shortly afterwards, the funeral director came in. He presented Pa with what looked like a fun-size cereal packet. 'My condolences, Mr Breeze,' he said. Pa nodded and quickly left. Once outside, he turned his back to us and opened the packet. For several seconds he inspected its contents, touching the ashes with his index finger. Then he began walking back towards the car and Rosie and I ran down the slope ahead of him and impatiently clicked the handles of the doors of the station wagon. He leaned backwards from the driver's seat to unlock the doors. He placed the packet of ashes in the dashboard compartment along with the Kleenex packet and the road maps and the can of engine oil and started the car. Then he switched off the engine and sat there without a word.

After long minutes of silence, he looked at us. 'I want you kids to stay here. And I mean it.'

He retrieved the packet and stepped out and walked down the leafy road and around the bushes at the corner of the block. He thought that we could not see him through the intervening undergrowth; but we could. We could see everything. Looking around to make sure he was unwatched, my father was rapidly sprinkling the powdery leftovers over the flowerbeds that ornamented the sidewalk – were they rose-bushes? Whatever they were, I had seen it with my own eyes: my mother reduced to fertilizer.

It's incredible – her sheer nowhereness.

17

The train has stopped again. This time we're in the outskirts of some town, with a view of clothes lines, underwear and gardens full of bathtubs, shopping trolleys, bits of wood and other junk.

'Are we there yet?' the woman asks.

The man sighs from behind his newspaper and I notice the sports page splash: WE'LL BE BACK, VOWS UNITED BOSS. 'Not yet, madam,' the man says. 'I'll tell you when we are.'

'I don't want to be late,' she says. She fiddles with her bandage, revealing an eyeball of pure red. 'It's my dog, you see.'

The man looks out of the window. 'I mean, this really is quite extraordinary. What possible reason could there be for stopping here?'

A minute passes. 'That's it,' the man says. 'I'm lodging a complaint. One simply can't take these things lying down.' He opens his briefcase and takes out a pen and a piece of writing-paper. He clicks down the point of the biro, places the paper on his briefcase, which he balances on his knees, and starts writing.

A few moments later, he puts his pen down and stands up. 'Would you keep an eye on my stuff?' he asks, and I nod.

I cannot resist looking at the letter, which is still on the briefcase.

Dear Sir or Madam . . . The paragraph that follows is scribbled out, as is the paragraph below that one.

At least that's one letter Pa will no longer have to deal with.

He was flummoxed by the pulverization of his friend.

'I don't know,' he muttered, as we drove back from the crematorium, 'I just don't know.' He clenched and unclenched his mouth and unrhythmically drummed his fingernails against the window. 'What does it all mean? I mean . . .' He stopped speaking, struggling with his feelings, ashamed about burdening me, an innocent whom he had brought unconsulted into the world, with his doubts. Perhaps, too, he was afraid of what my answer might be.

We reached the pacific streets of the Birds' District, passing a playground with see-saws and a sandpit where mothers pushed tots skywards on the swings and supervised their gleeful experiments on the slides with the sweet tug of gravity. On an impulse, I pulled over at the supermarket and, while Pa waited in the car, loaded up a trolley with loaves of wholemeal bread, eggs, a kilo of apples, butter, beers, ready-made mixed salad, Brie, mature Cheddar, salami, oranges, cans of soup, toilet paper, tomatoes, two rump steaks, minced meat, onions and bananas. Stuff he liked. And when we got home I made him a sandwich and a cup of coffee, and while he took it easy I filled up the dishwasher, cleaned the kitchen and stocked his fridge.

Then I checked the mailbox. A large brown envelope stamped with the Network logo fell to the floor.

I handed it to Pa, who was sitting at the dining-table.

He dropped it on the table and pushed it away. 'It's Paddy Browne's report. I don't want it. I've had it with them. They can keep their rubbish. I don't want to hear from those people ever again.'

'What about your action for reinstatement? Are you just going to let that drop?'

'It's over, John. Can't you understand? It's over. There's nothing I can do about it.'

I was suddenly angry. 'What happened to your fighting talk? Are you just going to let them walk all over you?' I tore open the envelope.

The covering letter said, *Dear Gene, Herewith a copy of the report which you requested. I hope that all is well. Yours, Paddy.* I picked up the enclosed booklet. 'Here we go, it's a copy of – '

After a moment, Pa said, 'What's the matter?'

I passed him the booklet. The authors of the report were identified on the front. 'Bear Elias,' Pa read out.

He looked at me and winked involuntarily with his lazy eye.

He said, 'You don't think that Angela . . . Surely, she . . .'

I pointed. There was her reference number at the foot of the last page, AF/103/2.

It was Angela who had fired Pa.

Pa removed his glasses from the reddened ridge of his nose and began pressing and kneading his brow with his fingers, as though desperately trying to reshape the contours of his skull. 'She was only doing her job,' he said finally.

I felt too guilty to reply.

He picked up the report and thumbed at its pages. He raised the silver of his eyebrows, curved faintly on his brow like moons in daylight, and pointed at some coloured pie charts. 'What did I tell you? Paddy Browne.'

Paddy Browne, Pa's worst enemy, and Angela, a virtual member of the family, a *de facto* Breeze, collaborating intimately and secretively to produce a report of this kind.

The bitch. The fucking bitch. So that's what she'd been doing Sunday night – while I, like an idiot, rotted in her flat, fearing the worst.

I pictured it: in the early hours of the morning, Angela sits flashing her fingers at the word processor with her long brown hair tumbling over her shoulders while Browne, his jacket long since discarded, informally brings her a cup of coffee to keep her going. He makes a humorous remark to which she replies, refining his joke in the special bantering manner which they have developed over weeks of teamwork; he, in turn, takes the joke one step further, and they both start tittering, delighted with themselves and each other.

I felt nauseous. How could this happen? Why hadn't she pulled out of the project?

A fresh wave of nausea. Surely the report was the full extent of their collaboration? Surely the Sunday all-nighter was purely professional? Surely there was no possibility of a double betrayal, of Angela and Browne . . .

I said, 'I don't understand it, Pa. I had no idea. She never told me.'

He was facing away from me towards the garden. Bushes were in blue blossom now.

I lit a cigarette. Jesus, she was hard. She was so hard.

Suddenly I was afraid.

Pa said, 'We were going to take up golf. And travel – we were going to do a lot of travelling, see the world. We had plans. You kids would be standing on your own two feet and we would have the time.' He was facing away from me and the backs of his ears loomed in profile from his head. 'You see, we were a team,' he said. 'We did everything together.' He caressed the table with his hand. 'She should be here with me right now. I wouldn't give a damn about any of this if she were here. But she isn't,' he said, amazement in his voice. 'That's the truth. She's gone. That's what's happened. This is it, you see. She's actually gone.'

He cleared his throat. I could not say anything. He was telling the truth.

There is a noise: it is my fellow traveller, returning with a cup of coffee. He takes a sip and places the plastic cup on the ledge beneath the window and sits back.

The train jogs. We're under way again, moving along with a thin clack of the wheels.

'Look,' he says, almost speechless. I do: the coffee in his cup is trembling so violently that drops have spilled on to his briefcase, staining his letter. 'It's unspeakable,' he says. 'Simply unspeakable.'

I make a sympathetic face, but then I leave in order to have another cigarette. This time I push down a window in the train corridor and lean out on my elbows, the smoke from my cigarette disappearing instantaneously in the train's envelope of wind.

It was early evening by the time I returned from Pa's, and a pile of pink sunlight broke into the hallway when I opened the front door. I walked through to the sitting-room. An attempt to clear up had been started but then abandoned. Steve, a crumb-filled plate on his lap, was at full-stretch on the sofa, poring over the latest junk mail – a religious missive entitled 'Who Really Rules the World?'. On the cover was a picture of the earth held like a cricket ball by an enormous white hand, the index finger taking a grip like a spin bowler's on a ridge of Asian mountains. I took a look at the pamphlet. Satan governed the world, it explained. *There is no need to guess at the matter,* it asserted, *for the Bible clearly shows that an intelligent unseen person has been controlling both men and nations.*

I handed Steve back the pamphlet. Looking at him sprawled

out there, I couldn't help feeling a soft gut-punch of disappointment. His famous citizen's arrest had not given him the push which, I had fleetingly dreamed, was all that he required to propel him into action. My error was clear: I had wrongly assumed that Steve's position in life was, in its relentless quiescence, like that of the schoolboy's classic example of latent energy, the static boulder perched on the top of the hill, shown in the diagram with arrows pointing downhill to demonstrate the rock's potential to rumble down the slope and transform its stored power into kinetic energy. But Steve was not ready to roll, a one-man landslide waiting for that happy impetus which would send him careering down the slope of achievement; he was flat-out on the sofa like a cracked slabstone in a skip.

In the kitchen, meanwhile, Rosie was making coffee for one.

A seen-it-all-before feeling came over me. It wasn't anything so mystical as *déjà vu*; it was the letdown that comes with the recognition of unprogressable circumstances which, like unceasing encores of a terrible performance, will recur and recur.

I soldiered on. 'I've been to Pa's,' I said to Rosie.

'How is he?' she said.

I dropped into a chair. 'Not great,' I said. 'Merv's cremation has really knocked him out. I left him in bed. He's thinking about Ma.'

I didn't say anything about Angela. Rosie was liable to go over to her flat and throw bricks though all of the windows.

I pushed my feet forward into some of that pink dusk light lying around on the floor. 'When are you going to see him?'

'I will,' Rosie said irritably. 'I'll phone him tomorrow.'

'Why tomorrow? That's what you said yesterday. It's always tomorrow. Why not today? I mean, I don't understand you. Why don't you just give him a call now and get it over with?'

'Oh, stop whining,' Rosie said, sitting on the sofa. 'Move over, Slug,' she said, rapping Steve's shins sharply with her knuckles. 'Ow,' Steve complained, and withdrew his legs. Rosie took a sip from her coffee, lit a cigarette and, ostensibly aiming at the plate which he held on his lap, flicked the ash on to his trousers. 'What's on TV?' she said.

Something had to be done.

I picked up the phone and rang the dogs' home. Trusty had not made an appearance, they told me.

Rosie said, 'Trusty's missing?'

'Yes. Since Sunday.'

'What, you mean she's run away?'

'That's right. You'd know about it if you bothered to speak to Pa.'

'Trusty,' Rosie said, sobbing suddenly.

I said, 'Jesus, Rosie, don't do that. Not now. I can't take that bullshit right now.'

Steve said, 'Johnny, that guy rang for you again. Mr Devonshire. Oh, yes, and you got some mail from him, too.'

I got up and walked out into the street and kept going. Run, Johnny, a voice in my head was telling me. Run.

In a daze, I walked aimlessly for an hour, past hamburger bars, West Indian restaurants, drink shops, drugstores, trees, cars, Pakistani grocers, pubs and travel agencies, past houses and more houses, past underground stations. I walked through a park and a housing estate, past a roundabout with signs pointing the traffic in every direction possible and then down towards the shore, the beam of the lighthouse beginning to swing over the city as the darkness encroached from the east.

Half-way down to the shoreline, I stopped and sat on a bench. Where to? The Foreign Legion? The sea? The west? The circus?

Two huge seagulls floated down to the ground in front of me.

I got on the bus to the Birds' District.

Pa was upstairs when I arrived, and I didn't disturb him. I sat alone in the living-room and drank a beer with the television switched on.

I noticed, on the floor beneath the table, the Bear Elias report.

Hadn't Angela realized what this would mean? Did she really think that she and I could go on as before?

Of course not. She wasn't stupid. She had known all along what the consequences would be.

There was only one conclusion, then. She wanted the consequences. She wanted the damage.

Well, fuck her. *Fuck* her.

I climbed up the stairs and knocked on the door of my father's bedroom and entered. He was not asleep. He was lying on his side, staring as though in a transfixion at the space between the bed and the cupboard. I looked at his limp palm and imagined it helplessly grabbed and squeezed goodbye by the huge golden hand of the Network.

'Can I get you anything?' I said. 'A cup of tea?'

One eye flicked in my direction and locked there.

An unventilated reek reached my nostrils. On the floor, trails of unwashed clothes led to the crammed laundry basket. There, crumpled at the foot of the bed, was his referee's shirt.

I stooped to the ground and picked up an old newspaper. I sat on the edge of the bed and turned the pages. 'I was thinking,' I said, 'that I might be getting myself a job.' This was not strictly true, of course, but I could think of no other way of bringing up the subject. I glanced at him. His eye was still unblinkingly pointing at me from the corner of his face, like the eye of a fish. I came to the appointments pages. Warehouse manager. Quality supervisor. Construction superintendent. Development manager. Mechanical engineer. Team leader, housing support staff. Seasonal ranger. Nothing for which Pa, with his twenty-five years plus in the railways, was particularly qualified.

'There are plenty of jobs here which you could do in your sleep,' I said. 'With your experience – '

'Stop fooling around, John,' Pa said, his voice half muffled. 'I'm not a baby. I don't need mollycoddling.'

'I'm not mollycoddling anybody,' I said. 'I'm serious. This is a big opportunity for you to do all those things which you've always been interested in.'

'I'm fifty-six years old. It's finished. It's the end of the road.' He pulled the bedspread over his cheek.

'What are you talking about?' I said. 'You've got a lot to offer. Why don't you join one of those executive job clubs? Or sign up with a head-hunter?'

Pa suddenly twisted around and looked directly at me.

'*Head-hunter*? Where do you think we are, Borneo?' He laughed sourly. 'You look for a job, if you want to,' he said, falling back on to the mattress. 'As a matter of fact, it's about time you did. I've given it some thought. The days of subsidizing your activities are over. The money simply isn't there any more.' He rolled further over, showing more of his back to me. 'You're on your own now, Johnny. I'm through with working my guts out just so that you and your sister can live for free. You're going to have to stop feeling sorry for yourself and go to work like everybody else.'

'I know that,' I said.

He continued as though he hadn't heard me. 'You sit there moping around all day waiting for I don't know what, inspiration, as though some angel is going to come down and make those chairs for you. Doing nothing, that's what it comes down to. Meanwhile, I'm bankrolling you.'

'I told you,' I said. 'I know, and I'm going to look for work. I'm going to pack in the chairs. There's no need for you to pay anything.'

'Oh, no? What about the flat? Who's going to pay for that? You think I've forgotten that you're supposed to be paying rent for that?'

I said nothing.

'Johnny, all I'm saying is, time's up. Welcome to the real world.'

'OK, OK,' I said irritably, rising from the bed. 'And what about you? What are you going to do?'

'I've finished with the whole racket. The whole thing can go on without me.'

'For God's sake, Pa,' I said.

'For *God's* sake?' He hurled back the bedcover and sprang out of bed in his underwear, the straps of his vest loose on his shoulders. 'What do you mean, for *God's* sake?' He pointed furiously at the ceiling. 'You think He's interested in any of this? You think He gives one single damn?'

Suddenly self-conscious, he flattened his hair with his hand and pulled up a vest strap.

'I've got to go,' I said, as he started to speak.

I went on my own to a bar by the quays and drank beer and

angrily and fearfully thought about Angela, trying, as one drink followed another, to think of a way through all that had happened, to conceive of a turn of events by which the present mess would be left behind and she and I would emerge together, in a different and hopeful place, united. I couldn't.

I also thought about my father. His problem was simple. He was suffering from overexposure to truth.

I thought, Join the club, Pa.

I was drunk by the time I got home. Rosie and Steve were in bed. I walked through the wreckage of the sitting-room to switch on the television; on top of it was a large manila envelope franked by the Devonshire Gallery. I ripped it open. A glossy brochure fell out.

It was entitled 'THE FALLEN – Five chairs by John Breeze'. On the left page were two brightly lit photographs of my chairs lying on their sides and casting a dramatic amalgam of shadows. On the right page was a text.

Common, in these oblique – some would say bleak – times, are creations the chief, indeed sole, purpose of which is purportedly to illustrate or exemplify an ideology or thought, no trace of which, alas, is discoverable in the work itself. Thus the vehicle of art, hitherto harnessed to truth and beauty, is hijacked by charlatans, attention-seekers and fraudsters of numberless variety and steered to destruction. This banditry is most harmful in its obscuration of that handful of artists who, unlike the aforesaid impostors, infuse their work with a genuine intellectual and moral content. From time to time, however, there arrives a talent so distinctive and so self-evident that no bogus overshadowing is possible. Such is John Breeze.

These five fallen stools are, first and foremost, beautiful. The graceful steel legs, evocative, perhaps, of the animal world, and the perfect maple seats, individual yet familial, are harmonious and apt. But it is the dimension of veracity which makes these objects other, and more, than furniture. For, while exhibiting every appearance of balance – the tripod is the most ancient and trusty of stands – the chairs cannot remain upright. Raise them up and time and again they tumble to the ground. The result is both true art and art that is true. The fallen, futile stools, pathetic and dysfunctional, at once flawed and possessed of perfection, are the interrogative, unmistakable icons of our very selves.

S. D.

I pocketed the brochure in my jacket. In the middle of the night I awoke on the sofa, drank cold water from the kitchen tap for thirty seconds, and hauled myself to bed.

18

I was awoken on Thursday morning by Rosie's loud voice. 'Come on,' she was saying. 'Get dressed, we're going.'

'What? What time is it?'

She pulled open the curtain. 'Time to get up.'

'What do you think you're doing?'

Rosie pulled a face. 'God, it smells in here.' She opened the window. 'We're going to cheer up Pa,' she said, 'by treating him to brunch. I've done all the shopping.'

I said, 'Close the window, will you, you'll let in the flies.'

I pulled on some clothes, lit a cigarette and went barefooted into the living-room.

There had been a transformation. The carpet was clean, the sofa cushions had been plumped, a fresh bunch of daffodils stood pertly in a transparent vase. Even the jam-stains on the wall had been washed down to a pale raspberry shadow.

'Bloody hell,' I said.

'Steve did it,' Rosie said. 'He got up early and did it all by himself.'

Steve was standing at the door of the kitchen, bashfully scratching his neck. 'Well, this is great,' I said. 'I'd forgotten how nice this place can look.'

'Get some shoes on,' Rosie said, picking up a full carrier bag and handing it to Steve. 'The cab's here.'

Rosie paid the fare. 'Pa, it's us,' she shouted as she opened the front door. She went into the kitchen. 'This place is disgusting. Look at the cooker, look how greasy it is.' She removed the gas rings and began to wipe the surface. 'Now leave, all of you. Steve, go mow the lawn. John, you go get Pa. Tell him brunch will be served in ten minutes. And set the table. Use the silver.'

I found my father by the window in his towelling dressing-gown, looking down at the garden. I went to stand next to him, and shoulder to shoulder we watched Steve bringing the old mower on to the lawn, the blue-painted blades splashed with rust. Even though the grass was long, in Steve's hands the mower travelled fluently over the ground, each noisy forward drive rhythmically giving forth a full spurt of cuttings, each drawing-back making the same high wheeze. He turned around at the holly tree and, accompanied by the machine's rich summery rattle, in one continuous movement swooped towards the house over the path he had just cut.

Pa sighed. 'I'll be there in a minute,' he said, still looking out.

Downstairs, I unflapped the white table-cloth, decking it out with the silver cutlery which had come down from my mother's parents as a wedding present. Rosie entered with small purple flowers and put them in a vase on the table. 'Not like that,' she said, adjusting the position of the knives and forks. 'Like this.'

By the time Pa descended, now wearing stripy pyjamas under his dressing-gown, the table was crammed with pots of marmalade and strawberry and blueberry jams, with cartons of orange juice and grapefruit juice, croissants, *pains au chocolat*, a pot of coffee, boxes of branflakes and cornflakes, a jug of milk, a full toastrack and white plates festooned with strips of smoked salmon. A crazy, excessive spread. 'Sit down, Pa,' Rosie said, unfolding his napkin and inserting it into the neck of his pyjama shirt.

'I'm not really hungry,' Pa said as she left for the kitchen. 'I'm never going to be able to eat this.'

Rosie returned with a panful of scrambled eggs which she heaped on to Pa's plate, then ours. Then she served up sausages and bacon.

'Now,' she said, 'let's tuck in.'

Our father looked with dismay at his plate, then began picking weakly at the soft rubble of his eggs. Rosie poured him a glass of grapefruit juice. 'Drink this,' she told him.

He took a mouthful.

Rosie said to Steve, who was wolfing down an entire piece of buttered toast, 'Stop making that noise.' She looked at me. 'What are you waiting for? Start eating.'

We all ate.

We needed something to talk about. I rose from the table and brought back the Devonshire brochure, which was still in the pocket of my jacket. 'Here,' I said to Rosie. 'Something to make you laugh.'

'What's this?' she said, beginning to read, and then a smile appeared on her face. She started to chuckle, then coughed on her food. She swallowed and shouted, 'I don't believe it. I just do not believe it.' She was laughing uncontrollably. 'Pa, look at what your brilliant son has done.'

Pa read. He tapped the paper when he had finished. 'Is this it? Is this what your exhibition is?'

I said, 'This wasn't my idea, Pa. It was Simon Devonshire's. I had nothing to do with it.'

Pa said, 'Do you believe this stuff? Do you really think' – he paused to quote – 'that we're "pathetic and dysfunctional"?'

Rosie said, 'Johnny, I never knew you were so deep.' Her elbows banged against the table as she toppled forward with laughter. 'And there I was thinking you were just a nerdy little brother making crappy furniture.'

Pa was sitting there with an expression of bafflement. I said, 'Pa, you can't take this stuff seriously. It's just something which has been dreamed up by the gallery.'

Steve, who meanwhile had been reading the brochure, said, 'This is so depressing.'

Rosie said, 'Steve, we'd all appreciate it if you refrained from being stupid for about one hour. OK? After that you can go back to being dumb.'

'No,' Pa suddenly asserted. 'Steve's right. It *is* depressing. It's depressing because it's true.'

I said to Pa, 'I told you, it's all bullshit. It's – '

'It's bullshit, all right,' Pa said, 'but it's true. Bullshit is the truth.'

'What are you talking about?' I said. 'I tried to make those chairs properly. I didn't mean to make them like that.'

'Forget about the chairs, will you?' Pa shouted. 'I'm telling you, bullshit is right. Bullshit is what it comes down to. This is bullshit,' he said, gesturing at his gathered family. 'This breakfast is bullshit.' He was standing up now, tightening the belt of his dressing-gown, swaying slightly. 'Shut up, Rosie,' he said, as she opened her mouth to speak. 'You don't give a damn for months, then you come here and make a few sandwiches and a cup of coffee and everything is supposed to be fine. Jesus.' He pulled his napkin from his throat and threw it on to his food. 'I can't breathe. I need some air.'

He went to the french windows and, face aflame, struggled with the sliding door. It gave way with a loud crack.

The musical sound of the garden filled the room.

Rosie said, 'You've broken the window, Pa.'

Pa said, 'I want you all to go, please. Now.'

Rosie said tremulously, 'Right, we're leaving,' knocking her chair to the ground as she rose. 'Steve.'

I said, 'Come on, Pa, let's not fight like this. It's us.'

'*Us*?' He swivelled into a brawler's stance, legs apart and fists clenched. 'What's that supposed to mean? Who the hell is *us*?'

Rosie looked at me, frightened.

Pa said, 'Well? Well, Johnny? You're so smart, you're the one with all the hotshot ideas, what's the answer to that one?'

'I . . .' I said. 'Pa . . .'

Steve said, 'Look.' He was pointing into the garden.

It was the dog.

'Trusty!' Rosie shrieked, running out on to the lawn. She hugged the animal ecstatically and led her into the house. 'Steve, get a bowl of water, she must be parched.'

Claws clicking, tongue tipped out of the slack folds of her mouth, Trusty ran towards Pa, who had dropped into a chair, and jumped on to his lap.

He pushed her away roughly and she fell squarely on to her side with a yelp.

'How can you be so horrible?' Rosie shouted. 'Come here, Trusty, my darling.'

Pa said, 'If she's got pups inside her I'm putting them down. I mean it. I'm putting them down.'

'Here, Trusty,' Rosie said, putting a plate of sausages and eggs on the floor, 'here, my darling.'

'Don't do that,' Pa said. 'If you reward her now she'll just run away again.'

I saw an opportunity to laugh. 'Pa, not even Trusty would be so stupid as to run away for a week just for a plate of bacon and eggs. She gets that anyway, just by staying here.'

'Not for long she won't.'

'What do you mean?'

He sighed and closed his eyes. 'I'm thinking of selling up.'

'Selling up?'

'Selling this place, selling the flat. Selling up. Leaving.'

I hesitated. 'Where to?'

He sighed again. 'I don't know, son. Just leaving.' He opened his eyes. 'I need a change. I need . . .' He took a deep breath and said hoarsely, 'I don't think I can take it here much longer. Every time I see the garden, see those flowers, see that tree over there, that hedge even – I see your mother. Or I don't see her. That's the thing, you see,' he said, looking down. 'I don't see her. I just see a garden.' He snorted suddenly and put a hand over his face. 'I just see a garden . . .'

My sister ran over to Pa and held him. 'Pa,' she said, 'Ma hasn't gone, she's here, she's right here in all of us.'

He was sobbing now, both hands over his face.

Rosie looked at me furiously. Desperately, I said, 'Rosie's right. Ma . . . Ma's right here,' I said. 'With us.'

Pa was shaking his head. 'She's gone,' he said.

Rosie said, 'Pa, Pa,' and she kissed his pale head as his violent, liquid inhalations reported through the room.

We stayed that way for minutes: my father in tears, my sister hugging him, Steve and I just standing there miserably in the awful company of grief.

Eventually, there was an exhausted quiet.

Rosie passed him her handkerchief. 'Here, take this.'

He accepted it and covered his face with it, patches appearing on the cloth. 'I'm sorry, kids,' he said, wiping his eyes. 'I'm just tired. I've really been through the wringer this week. I'm sorry.' He blew his nose, then blew it again. He patted Trusty, who had finished eating. 'Good girl,' he said. 'Good girl.'

'I'll run you a bath,' Rosie said gently. 'Don't worry about breakfast, I'll clear it all up.'

'Thank you, my love,' he said. He gulped up mucus. 'I'm sorry for snapping at you like that. I don't know what's come over me.' He shuffled his feet into his slippers and got up.

'Thank you for mowing the lawn,' he said to Steve. 'You've done a great job.'

When he came down from his bath, shaven and dressed in his old track suit, he said, 'I'm taking the dog for a walk on the beach.' He picked up the leash and clipped it to the dog's collar. 'I'll see you all later. Thanks for the breakfast.'

The front door made a slam.

Rosie said, 'Poor Pa.'

I threw her a cigarette and lit one myself. We smoked together for a while without speaking. Then I came out with the news about Angela's role in Pa's sacking. I did not have the strength to withhold the information any longer.

She breathed in her cigarette in silence, regarding the elegant plumes of fumes that flowed from her mouth. Her short hair had been lightened by the sunshine of the last week. She said, 'You didn't know she was doing this? You really didn't know?'

I shook my head.

Instead of flying into a rage, she looked at me with curiosity and said, 'It's over between the two of you, isn't it?'

I shrugged weakly. 'I don't know. I don't know what's going to happen.'

'Well, think about it. How is she going to be able to deal with us? I mean, what does she expect us to do? Carry on being nice to her as though nothing had happened?'

'I don't know,' I said. I looked down at my shoes. The soles were splitting away from the leather.

She said softly, 'I can tell you one thing. I'm not speaking to that woman again.'

There was a thick gasp of blades snagging in grass: Steve had resumed his mowing.

Rosie stubbed out her cigarette. 'Cheer up, John. The two of you weren't going anywhere, anyway, if you want to know the truth. Water finds its own level.'

'What's that supposed to mean?'

'You're a miserable overgrown teenager, she's a successful businesswoman. That's what that means.' She began scraping the food left on the plates on to a serving dish.

I controlled my temper. 'You and Steve are hardly the ideal couple either,' I said.

She laughed and turned to look into the garden, where her boyfriend was disentangling grass from the machine. 'Look at him, the poor darling. Look at that frown on his face. He's not used to concentrating that hard.'

'He's a total idiot, that's why,' I said.

Rosie, who was holding a pile of plates, stiffened.

'Look, I'm sorry,' I said. 'But if you're going to start talking about my life like that, I can do the same about yours. Tit for tat, Rosie. I can't see why you should be the only one to speak your mind. Besides, it's the truth. It's not my fault that Steve's a waste of space.'

She turned to me with glistening red eyes, hugging the dishes to her chest, and said hoarsely, 'You think I don't know that? You think you need to remind me of that?'

I blushed. 'I – '

'What do you think, that I wouldn't get someone else if I could? That I'm turning down offers to stay with Steve? You think that I'm happy with the way things are?'

I kept blushing. 'I'm sorry,' I said.

She wiped her mouth with her sleeve and went into the kitchen before joining Steve in the garden. She held open a plastic bin-liner while he, wearing my father's old gardening gloves, filled it with handfuls of grass. When the bag was filled they set about weeding together, pulling nettles and other long-rooted intruders from the soil of the flowerbeds, clearing the garden of all blemishes.

I left them to wait for my father. He would be on the beach now, throwing sticks into the grey surf for Trusty to chase, or examining the stranded blue gunk of the jellyfish, or stepping along the black-rocked breakwaters that ran out into the water flanked by red triangular signs warning swimmers of dangerous currents. He would reach the tip of the breakwater and count the ships queuing on the horizon for entry to the port, marvelling, as usual, at the relentless forces of international trade, the thousands of smooth-running charter parties that gave birth to this traffic jam on the sea, and then he would turn around and look at the beach, where ramshackle bars on short stilts had sprung up for the summer. He would tramp the long way home, a mile over the cardboard-coloured edge of the land, then back through the wooded dunes, keeping an eye out for wildlife behind the barbed-wire fences – pheasants, rabbits, magpies, foxes. The dunes. I used to dig huts and erect tree-houses in those hills with my friends, secret camouflaged retreats where we kept comics and soccer magazines and, in case of emergencies, flashlights and bars of chocolate. They were our hideaways: a cool bolt-hole scooped out in the sand, or a construction up on a bough twenty feet in the air where you would sit with a branch in each hand for balance. Below, the Bird's District, with its neat red roofs and fat perfect trees, would be reduced to a toytown and Rockport itself to a tranquil gathering of towers and spires; above, as you lay horizontal and looked up, the blue, giddying sky. You'd feel like a stone at the bottom of the sea.

And here I am today, on this train now steadily hauling me, through flat, dark, green fields, to Angela.

When I think of her, I daren't think.

It was the same when I arrived home from the brunch. I fell on my bed, thought about Angela and felt nothing but fear.

I fell asleep and awoke at six. I took a shower, shaved and went into town, to the Devonshire Gallery.

I found Simon Devonshire sitting at his desk, drinking from a bottle of red wine. Behind him, in the unlit rear of the gallery, were the scattered shapes of my chairs on the floor.

'Well, well, well,' Devonshire said slowly. 'If it isn't John Breeze himself. Come in and have a drink.'

I was too embarrassed to do anything but accept the glass of wine he held up. 'I'm sorry I haven't been able to get back to you earlier,' I said.

He shrugged.

'And I'm sorry about the chairs,' I said.

'Sorry? Why?' He was examining his glass.

'Well, because . . .'

'Because what?' He raised himself vigorously. 'John, you have made a bold and pertinent statement with your chairs. You've broken new ground.'

'But – '

'No buts, John.' He touched a wall-switch, and the back of the gallery lit up like a stadium. 'Come over here, take a look at what we've done.'

I followed him to where the stools, as though skittled by some passing missile, lay randomly on the ground. He motioned with his arm. 'Here they are, my boy. *The Fallen*.'

I looked, even though there was nothing to see, nothing but objects that served no purpose other than to take up space. These were not even seats. These were useless, meaningless bits of matter.

'It's never going to work,' I said. 'You'll never pull it off.'

Devonshire laughed. 'Have faith, Johnny. If you tell people that these things are significant, bingo, they'll believe it. It's exactly what they want to hear, it's what they *need* to hear. Why else do you think they come?' He laughed again. 'No, they'll buy this all right. They'll be queuing up to buy these Breezes.'

I had not heard my pieces described in that way before – as Breezes.

Devonshire said, 'I want your co-operation on this, Johnny. I want your full co-operation. Do you follow me?'

'Yes, I do,' I said. I had no option.

'Excellent,' Devonshire said. He put his arm around my shoulder as he showed me to the door. 'You want to start believing in yourself,' he said. 'I promise you, these chairs of yours are wonderful. You've got talent, John, real talent.'

By the time I returned home it was evening, with red clouds scrawled to the west above the mountains.

Angela called at about nine o'clock. She knew that I knew.

'I'm sorry, Johnny, I'm sorry,' she said. She began to cry. 'I feel so terrible, I can't tell you how terrible I feel, Johnny.'

I could not say anything. My throat had dried up completely.

Angela sniffed. 'Just a moment,' she said, 'I'm just going to close the door.' She returned. 'Johnny, are you still there? Say something. Johnny? My love?'

'I'm here,' I said.

'Johnny, my love,' Angela said. She sniffed again.

There was a silence.

Then I said, 'Well, I don't know, Angie, I just don't know any more.' My voice was low and very calm.

Angela said, frightened, 'Johnny?'

Another silence.

Then she said, 'Johnny, I have to see you. Why don't you come here on Saturday? My parents are going to be away and we could go and stay at their place. It would just be the two of us.'

I said, 'You want me to drive all the way to you? All the way out to Waterville?'

Angela said quickly, 'No, I just, I just thought that . . .' She stopped. 'I'll come,' she said decisively. 'I'll get the train.'

'No, wait,' I said. I had to get out of the flat, out of Rockport. 'I'll come. I can't say when yet. I'll see you when I see you. At your parents' house.'

'Johnny?' Angela said. 'I'll be waiting for you, my love.'

That's right, I thought as I hung up, you bloody wait. You get a taste of what it's like.

I slept badly that night. I was worried about everything. I was worried about Angela and I was worried about Pa and I was worried about what I was going to do with the rest of my days. I was so worried about my life that I wasn't worried about dying.

19

The train is rumbling slowly forward. The lady is asleep, mouth open, nose upturned, lightly snoring. The man has cast aside his newspaper and is staring dispiritedly out of the window, his shoulder leaning against the side of the carriage. He has abandoned his coffee-stained letter of complaint, which lies crumpled on the floor, there being no litter bins.

'I might enter this quiz,' Steve said. This was yesterday, Friday, morning. Rosie had left for work and I was watching him watching TV while trying to cut his big toenail with a small pair of nail scissors. It was an unequal struggle, the blades flapping fruitlessly against the hard white outcrop. He was always grooming himself in public like this, filing his warts or picking his corns or pushing down his cuticles right in front of you. 'Bakelite,' he said to the television as he focused on his foot. 'I could win this thing,' he said. He put down the nail scissors and went to the kitchen to open the cutlery drawer. Returning with the large wine-coloured industrial scissors, he placed his foot on the edge of a chair and concentrated with a grimace. Crack: a solid fleck sprang across the room like a grasshopper. 'Riyadh,' Steve told the quizmaster

The phone rang.

It was Pa. 'Son, I wonder if you would come down to the tennis club with me this morning.'

'Yes,' I said, surprised, 'of course.'

'I'll be round in twenty minutes,' he said.

He hung up without further explanation, so I changed into tennis gear, white shirt and white shorts, and dug out an old wooden racquet with crooked cat-gut strings. Although tennis is not my game, I was happy enough to bat back a few balls to Pa. It was a positive sign of rehabilitation.

But when he arrived he was not in his sports gear; he was wearing his dark suit, a dark tie and clip-on shades over his glasses. 'Johnny,' he said falteringly, regarding me. 'Never mind. It doesn't matter. Don't bother changing. Let's get going, otherwise we'll be late.'

Late for what? I thought, but he was not saying anything. He just chucked me the car keys and fell into the passenger seat.

The tennis club, dreamily secluded in urban woodland, was just ten minutes away. I reversed into a parking space and looked to Pa for an indication of what to do next. He had not spoken during the journey, and now he just wound down the window and rested his elbow on the ledge and looked out at the surrounding scene. Through the brilliant and shadowy foliage you could see the soft orange terrain of the clay courts and the pale movements of players. The pick-pock of tennis balls being struck drifted through the trees. Pa took off his glasses, rubbed his eyes, then opened them wide and blinked hard, as though sleep still glued the lids together. Then he laid his head against the headrest and closed his eyes. A neat split had appeared at the exact centre of his flaking bottom lip. Apart from yellow-grey, that red gash was the only colour on his face.

Pa moved his head. A brown saloon had turned into the car-park. He sighed. 'Come on,' he said.

We stepped out. To my dismay, the saloon yielded the two Rasmussens, mother and son. Pa and Mrs Rasmussen kissed, and then she presented him with an object. Pa accepted it with both hands. It was a pewter urn and he held it by his waist like a bashful cup-winner.

Billy and I shook hands after a moment of hesitation. He must have wondered why I, a complete stranger to him, kept showing up at these most private and solemn moments. He must also have wondered what I was doing all in white, dressed for a spot of tennis.

Pa gave Amy Rasmussen his arm and they began walking.

'Merv was at his happiest here, when playing with your father,' Mrs Rasmussen said to me as I accompanied them. 'It was the highlight of his week.'

Pa led us through to the one unoccupied court. On each side, games were in progress. He looked at Mrs Rasmussen, who nodded. Then he looked at Billy, and I was prepared, after his jokiness in hospital, for an ill-judged one-liner. But Billy said nothing.

Pa removed the lid from the pot and said some words in a tired voice. 'Merv,' he said, 'was a fine man. He was a fine husband to Amy and a fine father to Billy. He was a fine friend to me. Merv was a loved man,' he said. He paused. The pause continued. 'May God rest his soul,' he blurted. In one decisive movement, he tilted the urn and spilled the ashes on to the back of the court, creating a small black and grey mound. Treading carefully, as though afraid to foot-fault, he scattered the rest of the ashes along the base line. Then he shook the pot into the air and the last particles of Merv came forth in a cloud and blew away in a drift of air. Out! shouted one of the players in the adjoining court. Pa crossed himself instinctively and we all remained where we were, contemplating the dust pile that the breeze was already dispersing.

A voice was raised in a shout. 'Oi! You there!' A man was approaching from the direction of the clubhouse. 'What do you think you're doing?' he demanded loudly, so that by the time he reached us people were watching. I guessed, from the broom he was brandishing, that this was the groundsman. 'You can't just come here and dump this dirt all over my courts.'

Pa said weakly, 'These ashes are Mervyn Rasmussen's.' He hesitated. 'He's a member here, like me. He came here a lot, you'd know him if you saw him.' Pa clumsily hunched his back in an attempt to trigger a memory in the groundsman.

'I don't care who you are,' the groundsman said, 'and I don't care who this rubbish is.' He began sweeping up the ashes towards the drainage ditch at the side of the court. 'This is my court and you don't put nothing on it, not without special permission'

Pa said, 'Please, don't, listen – '

Billy Rasmussen moved forward and snatched the groundsman's collar with his left hand and his wrist with the other hand, forcing him to drop the broom. 'Billy!' Mrs Rasmussen cried, 'don't!' Billy lifted the groundsman's small frame into the air, carried him forward and then threw him down hard beyond the doubles tramlines. Then he stepped towards the remains of his father and, knee-deep in a cloud of dirt, furiously kicked and stamped at the ash-heap until it had irrevocably scattered and petered out. 'Are you happy now?' Billy shouted at the groundsman. 'Is this what you want?'

All that was left of his father was a thin dustiness in the air above the court and black dust-stains on his clothing that a single low-temperature wash would remove. Billy turned and ran away across the courts, elbows beating like flippers, his champion swimmer's bulk ungainly in its movement over land.

My father escorted Mrs Rasmussen back to her car, and then he and I got into the Volvo. This time, he took the wheel.

After we had been on the road for a few minutes, I asked him whether I might have use of the car the next day.

'What for?' he asked.

It was a routine question, but I wished he hadn't asked it. 'I need to get to Waterville,' I said. I hesitated. 'To see Angela,' I said.

He didn't respond.

I felt I owed him an explanation. 'I need to see her. We need to talk about – '

'Take the car,' Pa said, cutting me short.

I said, 'I – '

'Take the car,' Pa said. 'I don't want to hear about it.'

We drove on. The day's brightness had turned my father's sunglasses almost black, obscuring his eyes. With his white shirt and dark tie, he almost resembled a secret serviceman.

We stopped at a traffic light and Pa reached up and opened the sunroof. He leaned back in his seat and tilted his head against the headrest, relaxing his neck muscles.

'It's green,' I said. 'It's green, Pa,' I said.

The Volvo lurched forward, then stalled as he mistimed the clutch. We caught the red again.

'I tell you, John, this car is in need of a service,' Pa said. He was sweating as the sunlight poured directly through the sunroof, and he wiped away a moustache of droplets with his sleeve.

He looked away, into his wing mirror. He said, 'John, I want to ask you a question, and I want you to answer me truthfully.' He coughed. 'You were there just now, you saw what happened to Merv.' He coughed again. 'Well, I've been trying to figure a lot of things out recently.'

'What is it, Pa?' I said.

'What I'm going to say may sound stupid, John. But I don't know what else I'm supposed to do.'

He adjusted his glasses in his embarrassment, then drove forward as the lights changed colour. 'Do you think – do you think that Merv, do you think, well, do you think that Merv will, I don't know . . . I mean, what's going to happen to Merv?'

He gave me a quick, anxious glance to see how I would respond. My poor father was deadly serious.

'I don't know,' I said, looking straight ahead. 'I think . . .' I stopped. 'I don't know,' I said.

'You don't think that, well, that it's impossible that, you know, Merv is alive elsewhere?'

I didn't answer immediately. I was thinking of heaven, the habitation of God and his angels and the beatified spirits, of a cloudland with a pearl-studded gate supervised by St Peter, of harp-playing, winged souls at immortal play, of cherubs and of the ninefold celestial hierarchy. What a limitless machine of fantasies was the human mind.

I said, 'Of course it's not impossible, Pa. Look up there,' I said, gesturing at the sun in the sky. 'Now that's impossible – a gigantic spinning ball of fire which gives life to a lump of rock millions of miles away. And yet there it is. What it's doing up there, I don't know, but it's there.'

'It is, isn't it?' Pa said.

I spoke with conviction. 'That's right. Everything is impossible, Pa, and yet everything is right here. Who's to say, if that sun is up there, that Merv isn't too?'

'That's true,' Pa said. 'You can never rule it out, can you?'

'I don't think you can,' I said, looking ahead.

We arrived back at the flat. He took his glasses off. His eyes were as red and dark as ever. 'Well, thanks for coming along, son. You've been a comfort to your old man.'

'No problem,' I said, stepping out. 'I'll see you tomorrow morning to get the car. You really don't mind?'

'Of course not,' he said. 'You do what you have to do.'

That night, Angela rang up.

'Hello there,' she said.

I was calm with tiredness. 'Hello,' I said.

'I – I just wanted to make sure you were coming,' she said.

'I'm coming,' I said.

She said nothing for a moment. 'Are you driving over?'

'Yes,' I said.

She said, 'What time do you think you'll be here? I don't want to rush you or anything,' she added quickly. 'I mean, get here when you can. Any time is fine for me.'

'Lunchtime, I suppose. Maybe a bit later.'

'That's fine. That's great.'

There was a noise as she moved. She would be sitting on the floor with her back against the wall, her feet neatly tucked together in front of her. She never made use of chairs.

She said, 'How is your father?'

'He's OK,' I said. 'All things considered.'

'That's good,' she said. There was another pause. 'I've always admired him, you know,' she said with feeling. 'I've always thought he has a wonderful outlook on things.'

'Right,' I said.

Angela said, 'We need to talk, you know, my darling. About us, I mean.'

'I know,' I said.

'This is horrible, John. I'm so sorry about everything.'

I didn't reply. Then I said, 'Well, I'll see you tomorrow, then.'

'Bye, Johnny. Bye, my darling.'

Steve turned in at about midnight and I stayed on alone in the sitting-room, watching television. I was too exhausted to go to bed and too exhausted to think.

I watched a sitcom, I watched a late-night chat show and then, as I was on the point of dropping off, a cartoon appeared on the screen. It was my old pal – old Wile E. Coyote.

It was the same old story, with Wile E. compulsively embarking on a succession of ruses which resulted in a succession of devastating own goals. But then something remarkable occurred. Disgruntled with his failed attempts at interception and entrapment, Wile E. Coyote decided to meet head-on the roadrunner's great advantage, speed, and to this end he procured a rocket, which he lined up in the direction of his prey. He then straddled the missile, ignited its fuse and, perched like bronco-buster, screamed successfully towards the roadrunner at great velocity; too successfully, in fact. The bird ducked and, overpowerful and unstoppable, the rocket propelled the coyote beyond the horizon and through the stratosphere and so deeply into outer space that our faint planet dwindled behind him to darkness. Then abruptly the rocket exploded like a firework, sending a shower of sparks into the black heavens, and the jinxed dog vanished into the nothingness. I contemplated the impossible: Wile E. Coyote, a goner?

Not so. The scintillations from the explosion settled into a grid of stars; a fresh constellation appeared in the night in the shape of a wolf with a bow.

I sat there in thrilled wonderment. He had done it. He had got out.

I went to bed uplifted.

I actually dreamed of Merv. I dreamed of him as a bunch of stars: the Hunchback with a Racquet.

The train is moving more smoothly now, sliding through the stony purple uplands that lie to the east of Waterville. We'll be there in less than twenty minutes. I'm glad, now that I'm here, that I allowed Pa to talk me out of coming by car.

I went to pick up the Volvo at about ten o'clock this morning. Trusty was dozing contentedly on the sofa, but he wasn't about. I went upstairs to his darkened room to find him: Pa?

No reply from the form in the bed.

There was a rough dawn as I pulled open the curtains. 'Right, come on, let's go.' I shook his dangling white leg, with its vandal's spray of burst veins. 'Come on, up we get. Come on, Pa.'

'No!' he said, erecting a brief tent as he kicked out under the duvet. 'Leave me alone!'

'You're going to get up,' I said, 'and you're going to get on with your life.'

'And do what?' he said, suddenly sitting up on his elbows and facing me, tassels of white hair shaking against his pink scalp. 'What do you suggest I do once I've got up?'

I had to invent something. 'I tell you what you're going to do,' I said, improvizing – and then it came to me. I went over to the heap of dirty linen and pulled out his referee's black shirt and shorts. 'You're going to put this on and you're going to get out there and take charge of a game. Look, it's a beautiful day out there.'

'You're crazy,' he said.

I disregarded him. I unfolded the ironing board and began to pass the steaming iron over the cloth, the wrinkles dissolving in its warm wake. 'Here we are,' I said when I finished.

'I don't feel like it,' he mumbled, his mouth against his mattress.

'That's not the point,' I said. 'Never say die, Pa, remember?'

'It's not that simple, Johnny.'

He was right, of course. 'Of course it is,' I said. 'Now get shaved and meet me downstairs in five minutes.'

He did not move.

I lit a cigarette and sat on the bed. 'What are you going to do, lie there for the next thirty years?'

'Why not?' Pa said. 'And it won't be thirty years either.'

'Come on, Pa,' I said. 'Be serious.'

'I am serious,' he said. 'Get this into your head: I've quit reffing. I've packed it in, like you said I should.'

I said, 'I'm not leaving until you're dressed. I'm being serious, too. I'll force you if I have to.'

Pa did not respond, so with one movement of the hand I whipped the bedspread away, exposing him there in his white underclothes. Kneeling on the bed, he furiously tried to wrench the duvet from my grip. He failed, and when I suddenly tugged hard I pulled him over the bed's two-foot drop to the ground. He fell on the sharp red tips of his elbows, then landed with a thump on his ribcage.

Breathing heavily, I said, 'Are you all right?'

He lay there groaning theatrically for a few moments, like an injured footballer; then, letting go of the duvet, he slowly raised himself.

'Are you OK?' I said.

He nodded his head, which he held tiredly in his hands as he sat on the bed. A small patch of damp showed on his Y-fronts by the tip of his penis. 'I'm not prepared. I can't go reffing just like that.'

'Sure you can.'

'You think so?'

'Of course. You'll run out on to that field and you'll be right into the swing of it.'

'But there isn't the time.'

'There is, if we get going now.'

He continued sitting there, rubbing his face.

'There's your kit,' I said, laying it out on the bed. 'And here are your boots.'

He looked expressionlessly at his shirt, at the nylon FIFA crest he had sewn on to the breast pocket. Slowly he took the shirt and pulled it over himself, head emerging first, then thin freckled arms. He leaned over and retrieved his special black water-resistant watch from the drawer by his bed and spent a full thirty seconds trying to tie it fast to his left wrist. After that he lifted his feet an inch or two from the floor and dragged his shorts up his legs, fractionally raising his behind to allow the shorts to arrive at the waist. Then he pulled on his socks.

I handed him his training shoes.

He laced them up automatically.

'Your boots,' I said, and he accepted the sports bag which contained them.

I led him into the car and drove him to the heath. I'd drop him off, then go on to Waterville. He'd get back on his own.

Out of the blue, on the way there, he began to chuckle.

'What is it?' I said.

'Man of the Month,' Pa said.

We both laughed.

'I always said he had it in him,' Pa said, and we laughed again, only this time our mirth was bellowing and unstoppable, every glance we exchanged bringing on still more laughter. I could barely drive I was laughing so hard.

'Watch it, Johnny,' Pa said, as we swerved narrowly past a parked car.

'Sorry,' I said. We drove on more slowly, still chortling.

'Is Rosie OK?' Pa said presently. 'I never know with that girl.'

'She's fine,' I said. 'She's just Rosie, that's all.'

He looked at me quizzically.

I said, 'She's fine, I said. I mean it.'

He reluctantly accepted my assurance. 'What about the flat?' he said. 'What's going to happen about the security?'

'Whelan came round this morning,' I said.

'He came round? Whelan came round?'

I smiled at his astonishment and relief. 'Yes, he did. I've got an estimate back at the flat.'

'New locks? Floodlights?'

'The lot,' I said. 'It'll be like Fort Knox once he's finished with it.'

Pa moved comfortably in his seat. 'I knew he'd come good. What did I tell you? Haven't I always said that Whelan is a man you can rely on?'

I looked to see if he was being humorous; he wasn't. 'I've never doubted it, Pa,' I said.

A moment later, formality in his voice, he said, 'There's something I've meant to say to you, son. Well done on the exhibition,' he said.

I smiled dismissively.

'No, you shouldn't be like that about it. It's no mean feat, what you've achieved.'

I did not respond. The odd thing was, I was actually beginning to feel the same way myself. The more I thought about it, the more it seemed that there was something meaningful about those chairs.

We drove up to the heath in the nick of time, the players erecting goalposts and crossbars and guying down orange goalnets into the grass for the last Saturday of the season.

I began to have misgivings. 'Are you sure you're going to be all right?' I said.

Pa unclipped his seatbelt and the ball of one bruised eye rolled towards the scene outside. Then he eased himself out of the car and put on his football boots. Sports bag in hand, he trod two or three times on the asphalt, studs clacking, before reaching the turf. Running slowly on the spot, he paused uncertainly as he surveyed the bright-shirted players suddenly springing up all over the sunny heath like miraculous desert flowers.

He looked back.

I gestured him onwards. Go on, I mouthed through the windscreen. Go on.

He came running back. 'Johnny, can you do me a favour?'

'What is it?' I said.

'I don't like you going all that way in the Volvo. There's something wrong with the engine, I know there is.'

'I'll be OK,' I said.

'I don't like it,' he said. 'You should take a look at yourself. You look washed out. It's a long drive, and I don't want what happened to Merv happening to you, that's all.'

I saw myself in the mirror: smears of dark blue under the eyes.

'Will you take the train? As a favour to me? Park the car at the station and leave the keys with Bill Dooley, the station manager.'

I sighed. 'OK, Pa. OK.'

'Thanks, son,' my father said.

He straightened and patted his shirt for his cards and notebook. He fished his whistle from his shorts pocket and hung it around his neck, then checked his watch and put his glasses away. 'Well, here we go, then, Johnny,' he muttered, shaking his legs and eyeing the teams splashing more and more colour over the heath as they assembled, trying to pick out a fixture which might require his services.

Like an alarmed creature of the prairie, he froze. He stood stockstill for three or four seconds, immobilized by some distant spectacle.

He walked forward for a few steps, making sure he was not mistaken. Then, without turning, he ran away like a boy towards the playing fields. He had found himself a game.

'We're almost there, madam.'

It is the man sitting across from me, and he wears an expression of happiness.

'Really?' the woman asks. 'Where are we?'

'This is Waterville now,' the man says. 'We'll be there in a few moments.'

He's right. I recognize those rooftops slewing by, the leafless overgrowth of the antennae.

A pang like a punch hits me in the stomach. She will have received the message I left on her answering machine and she will be at the station waiting for me. She will meet me as she always does, with a newspaper under one arm which she will toss into a bin as she walks up the platform, smiling at the ground, shapely in that blue-flowered dress she loves to wear on hot days, her ears decked out with marigold earrings, her ankles titillatingly unsteady in those shoes, those high ones – what do those high shoes look like again, exactly?

Wild ideas occur to me: pulling the emergency cord, hiding in the train until the coast is clear.

It won't work.

The train dips into the tunnel down to the station and darkens.

Holding fast to the luggage rack, I stand up in anticipation of arrival – and it is there again, the dizzying weightlessness I felt that night at her flat, hovering in her rooms like a man of air. Hitting some swerve in the rails, the train sways violently, and I'm hanging on to the rack as I'm swung around by the machine's huge straying energy. There is another swerve, but this time I'm ready for it, I'm riding with the shock; the tremor passes through me easily, as though I were not here.

The train gathers speed as the tunnel tilts still deeper into the earth. I still feel hollow and, all of a sudden, elated. I'm ready for her, for her and for all the circumstances that'll pass through in the way that they do, without care, without looking where they're going. Bring them on, too, what the hell, let's get it over with. Maybe it's a Breeze thing, to be vessels for the careless transit of events. Maybe we're built for it. Look at Pa, the hapless, steadfast bastard, look at how he's come through it all. Why shouldn't I be a chip off the same block?

My ears pop as the train begins to surface.

But anyway, you never know, things may turn out all right. You just never know.

That's right, isn't it?

The windows flash like spooks with daylight. Here we are, then. Here we go.

Also by Joseph O'Neill

Netherland

Longlisted for the Man Booker Prize 2008

A Richard & Judy bookclub pick

Winner of the PEN/Faulkner Award for Fiction

What do you do when your wife takes your child and leaves you alone in a city of ghosts?

Hans van den Broek chooses cricket. Alone in a terrorized city, struggling to understand the disappearance from his life of people, places and feelings, he seeks refuge in the game of his childhood. But New York cricket is a long way from the tranquil sport he grew up with. It's a rough, almost secret game, played in scrubby, marginal urban parks, by people the city doesn't see – people like Chuck Ramkissoon. Years later, when a body is pulled out of a New York canal, hands tied behind its back, Hans is forced to remember his unusual friendship with Chuck – dreamer, visionary, and perhaps something darker...

'Dazzling, told with great grace and daring'

KATE SUMMERSCALE

'Beautifully written' MONICA ALI

'Mesmerising. I've not read anything recently that has quite so brilliantly captured the exuberant madness and cultural diversity of [New York]' JEREMY PAXMAN

This is the Life

James Jones is slipping steadily through life. He has a steady job as a junior partner at a solicitors' firm, a steady girlfriend and a steady mortgage. Nothing much is happening in Jones's life but this is exactly the way he likes it.

Michael Donovan, meanwhile, is a star – a world-class international lawyer and advocate. Jones was once Donovan's pupil, but he left that high-powered world behind a long time ago. Then, out of the blue, Donovan contacts him; he has a job he needs Jones to work on . . .

Joseph O'Neill's debut is wonderfully clever and comic novel – about ambitions and aspirations and the realities that they inevitably collide with.

'Immensely well-written, original, inventive and readable'
Guardian

'An excellent debut, crisply written and full of dark observations of the fragility of worldly success' *Daily Telegraph*

'Fresh and funny' *Independent on Sunday*

'An engaging first novel' *GQ*

Blood-Dark Track

A Family History

Joseph O'Neill's grandfathers – one Irish, one Turkish – were both imprisoned during the Second World War. The Irish grandfather, a handsome rogue from a family of small farmers, was an active member of the IRA and was interned with hundreds of his comrades. O'Neill's other grandfather, a hotelier from a tiny and threatened Turkish Christian minority, was imprisoned by the British in Palestine, on suspicion of being a spy.

At the age of thirty, Joseph O'Neill set out to uncover his grandfather's stories. He emerged with a tale of two families and two charismatic but flawed men – a story of murder, espionage, paranoia and fear, and of human vulnerability to the violence of history.

'He uncovers fascinating parallels between the two men, illuminating the ways in which individual lives mesh with history'

Sunday Times

'This is a beautifully written and complicated book, in which difficult perceptions are expressed with forensic honesty'

Sunday Telegraph